The Three Stooges®

EBENEZER STOOGE

PRESENTED BY C3 ENTERTAINMENT, INC.

PAPERCUTZ™

The Three Stooges®

GRAPHIC NOVELS AVAILABLE FROM PAPERCUTZ™

ALL-NEW! FULL-COLOR GRAPHIC NOVEL!
The Three Stooges
BED-BUGGED!
PAPERCUTZ

THE THREE STOOGES #1 "BED-BUGGED"

ALL-NEW! FULL-COLOR GRAPHIC NOVEL!
EBENEZER STOOGE
PAPERCUTZ

THE THREE STOOGES #2 "EBENEZER STOOGE"

The Best of THE THREE STOOGES
AS GOOD AS NEW, HUH?
BOING

THE BEST OF THE THREE STOOGES COMICBOOKS: VOL. 1

BY NORM SAUNDERS
PETE ALVARADO
INTRO BY JOAN MAURER

The Best of THE THREE STOOGES Comicbooks
WHAT'S DA BIG IDEA MAKIN' US LOOK LIKE SUCH IDIOTS?
YEAH! YOU GOT US ACTIN' LIKE WE'RE A BUNCH OF KNUCKLE-HEADS!
RIGHT! WE'RE MORONS AND WE DON'T WANNA BE DRAWN AS ANYTHING BUT MORONS!

THE BEST OF THE THREE STOOGES COMICBOOKS: VOL. 2

BY NORM SAUNDERS
JOE MESSERLI

COMING SOON!

The Three Stooges
CELL-BLOCKHEADS
PAPERCUTZ

THE THREE STOOGES #3 "CELL-BLOCKHEADS"

DON'T TRY THIS AT HOME
PAPERCUTZ

THE THREE STOOGES #4 "DON'T TRY THIS AT HOME"

The Best of THE THREE STOOGES Comicbooks
OUCH!
YEAH!
BONG
UGH!

THE BEST OF THE THREE STOOGES COMICBOOKS: VOL. 3

BY NORM SAUNDERS

THE THREE STOOGES® graphic novels are available in paperback and hardcover from booksellers everywhere. THE BEST OF THE THREE STOOGES COMICBOOKS is available in hardcover only from booksellers everywhere.

Or order from us: please add $4.00 for postage and handling for first book, add $1.00 for each additional book. THE THREE STOOGES are each $6.99 in paperback, and $10.99 in hardcover. THE BEST OF THE THREE STOOGES COMICBOOKS are each is $19.99 each in hardcover only. Please make check payable to NBM Publishing. Send to: Papercutz, 160 Broadway, Suite 700, East Wing, New York, NY 10038 * 1-800-886-1223

www.papercutz.com

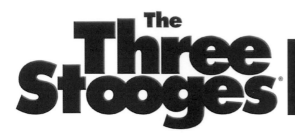

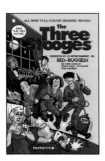

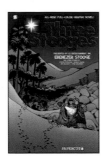

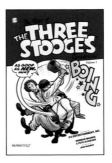

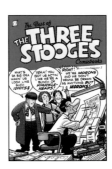

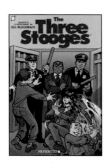

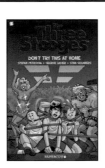

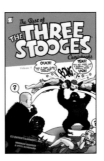

The Three Stooges®

#2
EBENEZER STOOGE

GEORGE GLADIR
STEFAN PETRUCHA
JIM SALICRUP · WRITERS
STAN GOLDBERG · ARTIST
LAURIE E. SMITH · COLORIST

Sister Mary-Mengele (Larry David)

PAPERCUTZ™
NEW YORK

The Three Stooges®
"Ebenezer Stooge"

"Ebenezer Stooge and the Gag of the M.A.G.I."
Script: Stefan Petrucha
Art: Stan Goldberg
Color: Laurie E. Smith
Lettering: Janice Chiang
"Bare Knucklehead Fighting"
and "Thrice Upon A Time"
Script: George Gladir
Additional Dialogue: Jim Salicrup
Art: Stan Goldberg
Color: Laurie E. Smith
Lettering: Janice Chiang

Production by Adam Grano
Associate Editor – Michael Petranek
Jim Salicrup
Editor-in-Chief

ISBN: 978-1-59707-336-3 paperback edition
ISBN: 978-1-59707-337-0 hardcover edition

September 2012 by New Era Printing LTD.
Trend Centre, 29-31 Cheung Lee St.
Rm.1101-1103, 11/F, Chaiwan, Hong Kong

Distributed by Macmillan

First Printing

Meet the Stooges...

Moe

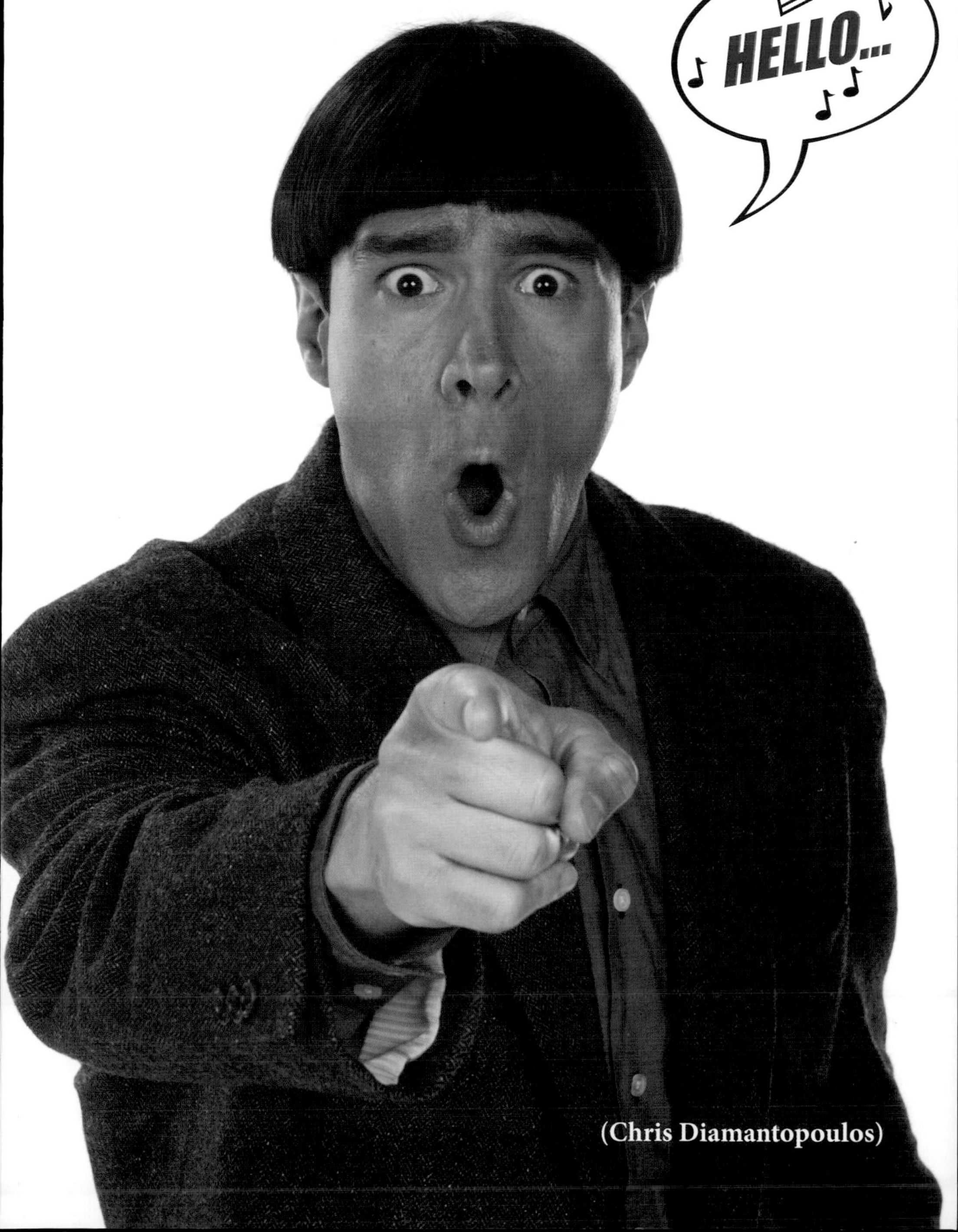
HELLO...

(Chris Diamantopoulos)

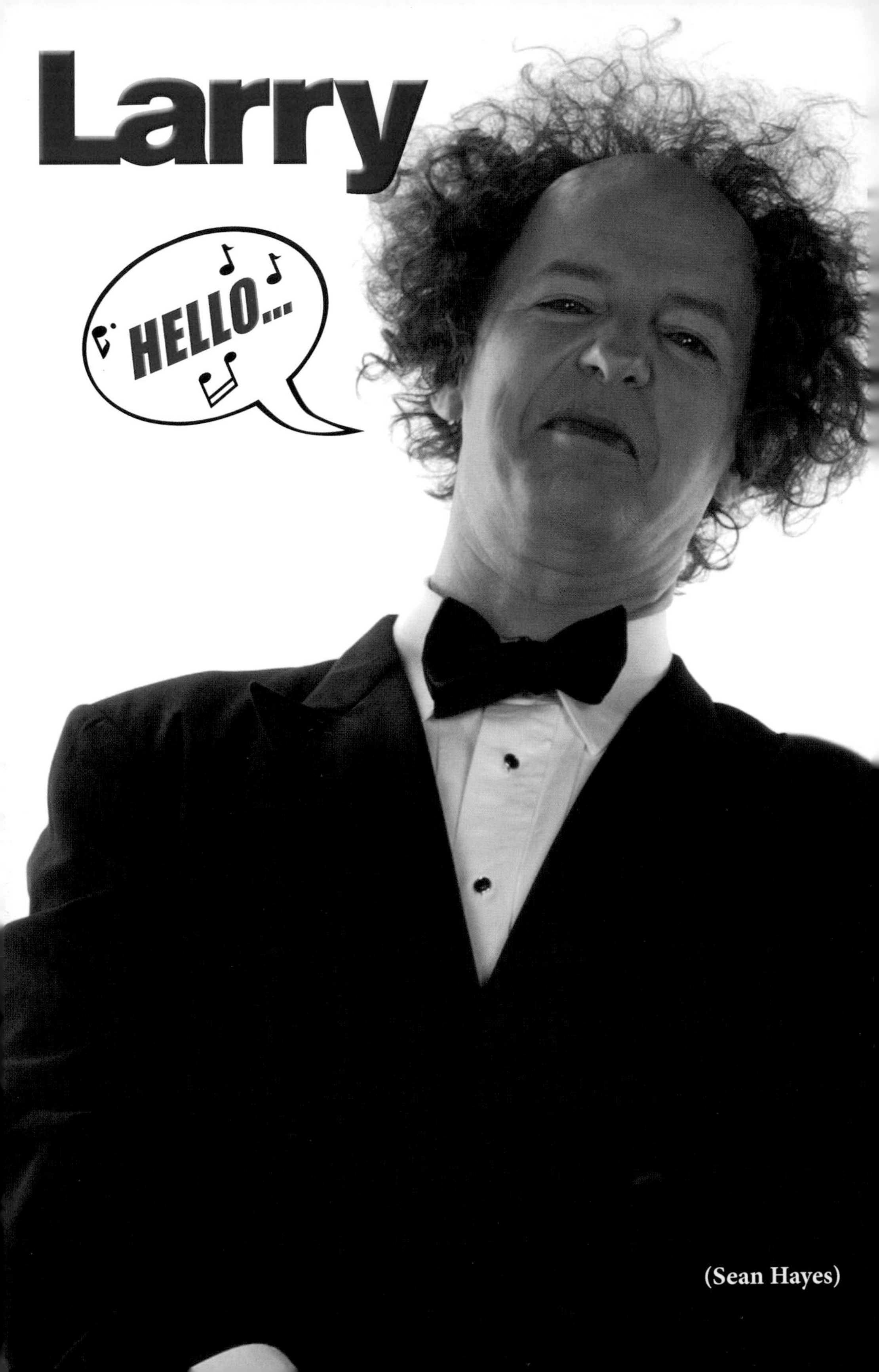
Larry
HELLO...

(Sean Hayes)

Curly

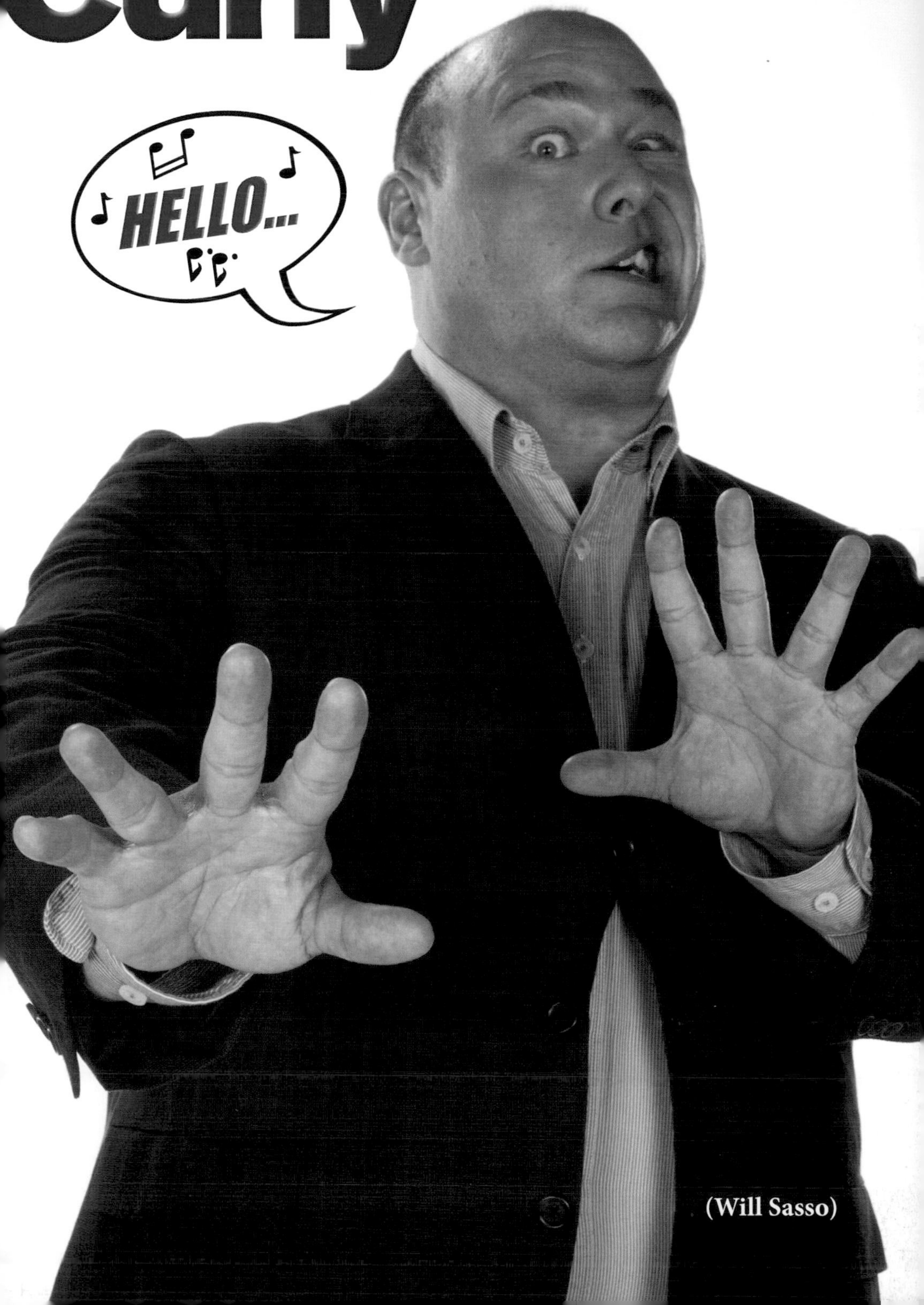
HELLO...

(Will Sasso)

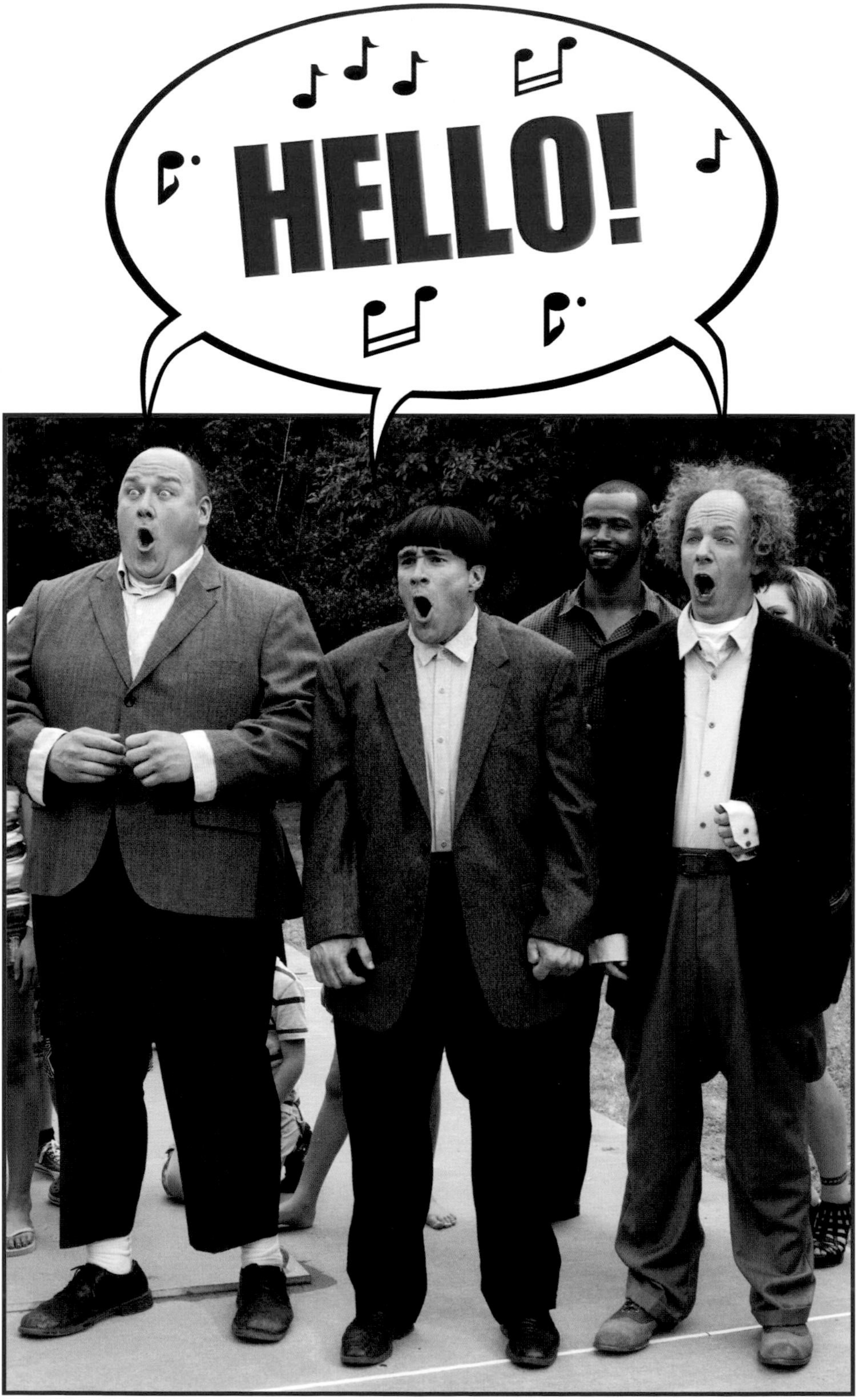
HELLO!

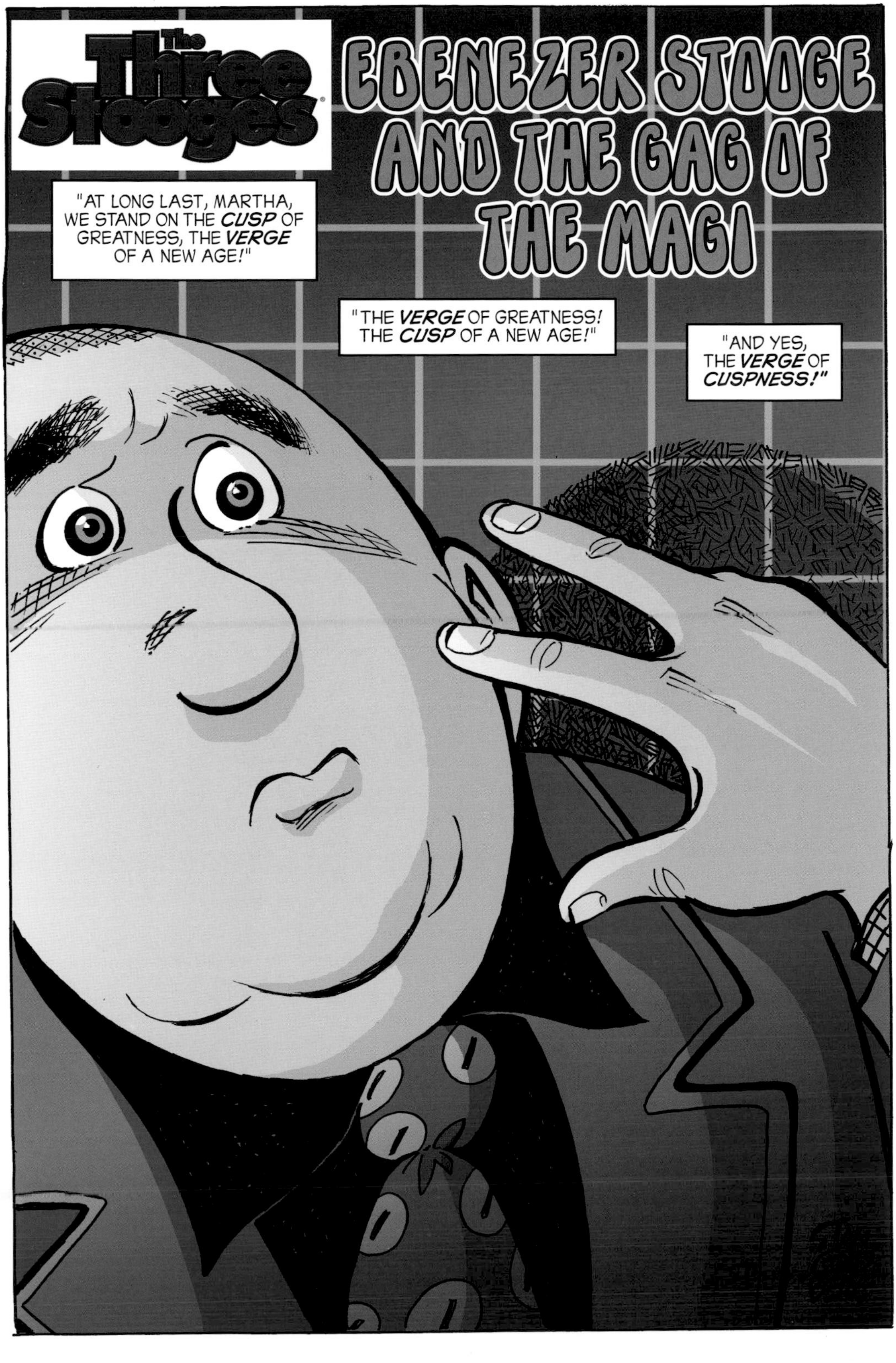
The Three Stooges
EBENEZER STOOGE AND THE GAG OF THE MAGI
"AT LONG LAST, MARTHA, WE STAND ON THE *CUSP* OF GREATNESS, THE *VERGE* OF A NEW AGE!"
"THE *VERGE* OF GREATNESS! THE *CUSP* OF A NEW AGE!"
"AND YES, THE *VERGE* OF *CUSPNESS!*"

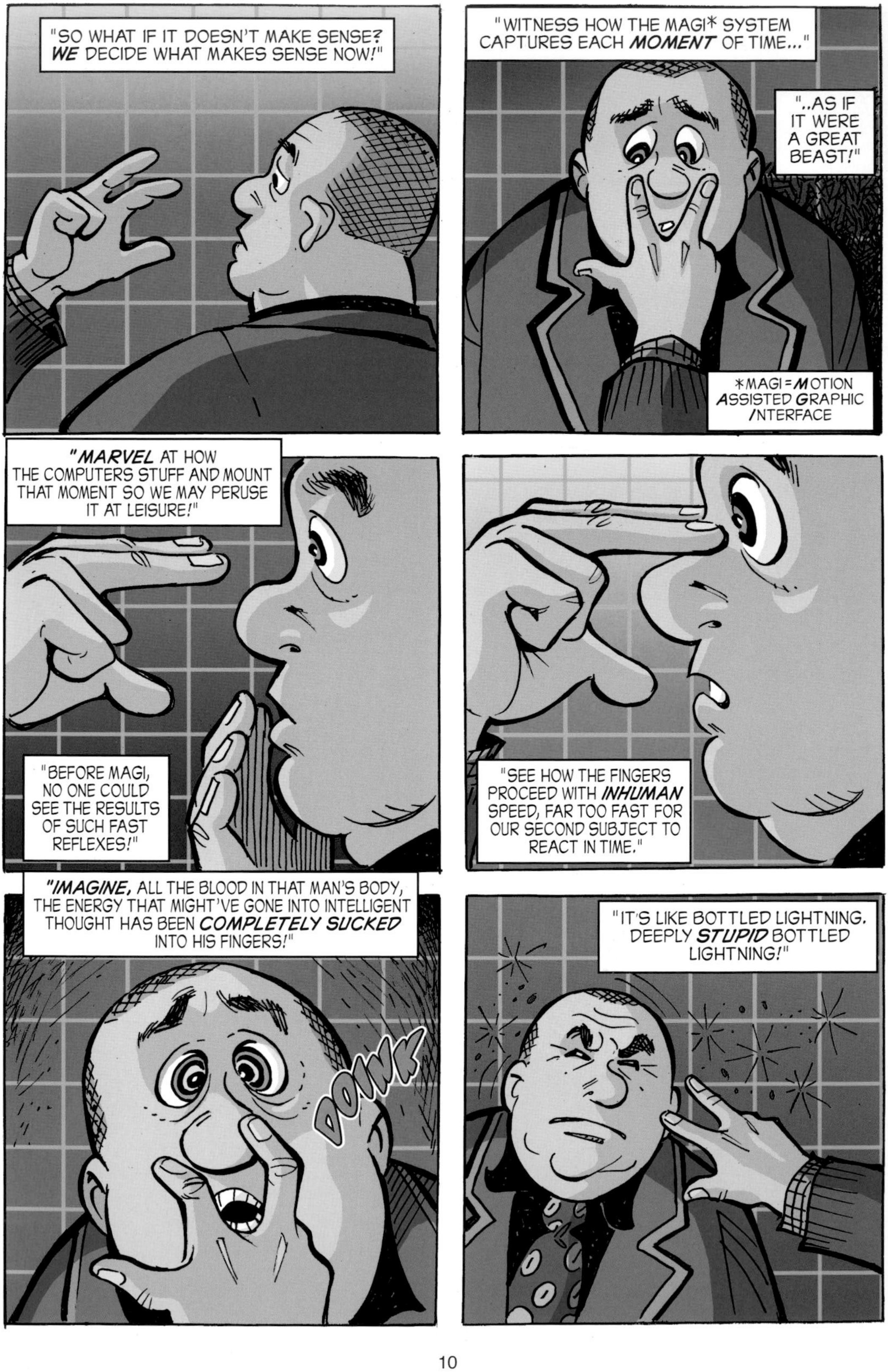
"SO WHAT IF IT DOESN'T MAKE SENSE? WE DECIDE WHAT MAKES SENSE NOW!"
"WITNESS HOW THE MAGI* SYSTEM CAPTURES EACH MOMENT OF TIME..."
"..AS IF IT WERE A GREAT BEAST!"
*MAGI = MOTION ASSISTED GRAPHIC INTERFACE
"MARVEL AT HOW THE COMPUTERS STUFF AND MOUNT THAT MOMENT SO WE MAY PERUSE IT AT LEISURE!"
"BEFORE MAGI, NO ONE COULD SEE THE RESULTS OF SUCH FAST REFLEXES!"
"SEE HOW THE FINGERS PROCEED WITH INHUMAN SPEED, FAR TOO FAST FOR OUR SECOND SUBJECT TO REACT IN TIME."
"IMAGINE, ALL THE BLOOD IN THAT MAN'S BODY, THE ENERGY THAT MIGHT'VE GONE INTO INTELLIGENT THOUGHT HAS BEEN COMPLETELY SUCKED INTO HIS FINGERS!"
DOINK
"IT'S LIKE BOTTLED LIGHTNING. DEEPLY STUPID BOTTLED LIGHTNING!"

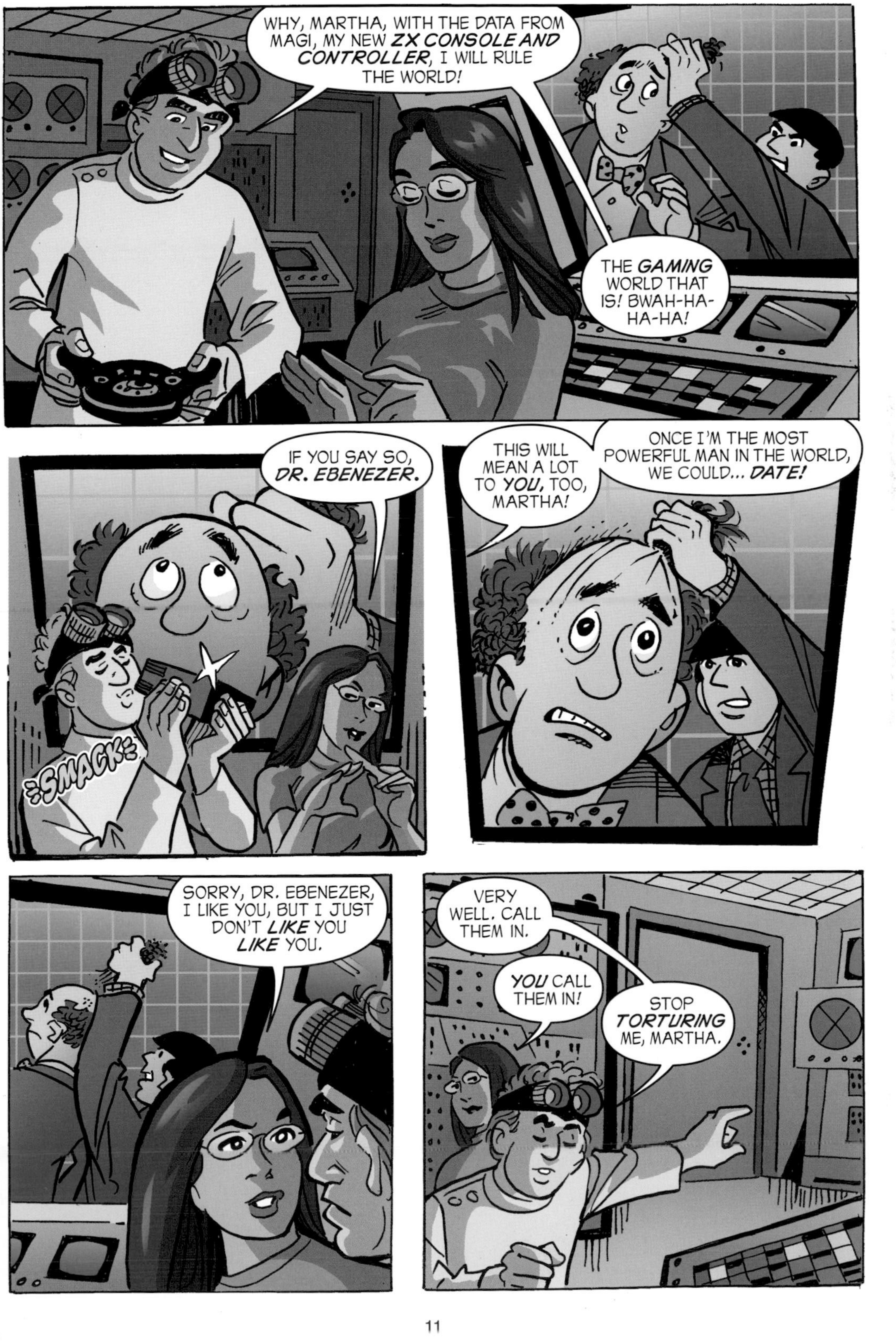
WHY, MARTHA, WITH THE DATA FROM MAGI, MY NEW ZX CONSOLE AND CONTROLLER, I WILL RULE THE WORLD!
THE GAMING WORLD THAT IS! BWAH-HA-HA-HA!
IF YOU SAY SO, DR. EBENEZER.
SMACK
THIS WILL MEAN A LOT TO YOU, TOO, MARTHA!
ONCE I'M THE MOST POWERFUL MAN IN THE WORLD, WE COULD... DATE!
SORRY, DR. EBENEZER, I LIKE YOU, BUT I JUST DON'T LIKE YOU LIKE YOU.
VERY WELL. CALL THEM IN.
YOU CALL THEM IN!
STOP TORTURING ME, MARTHA.

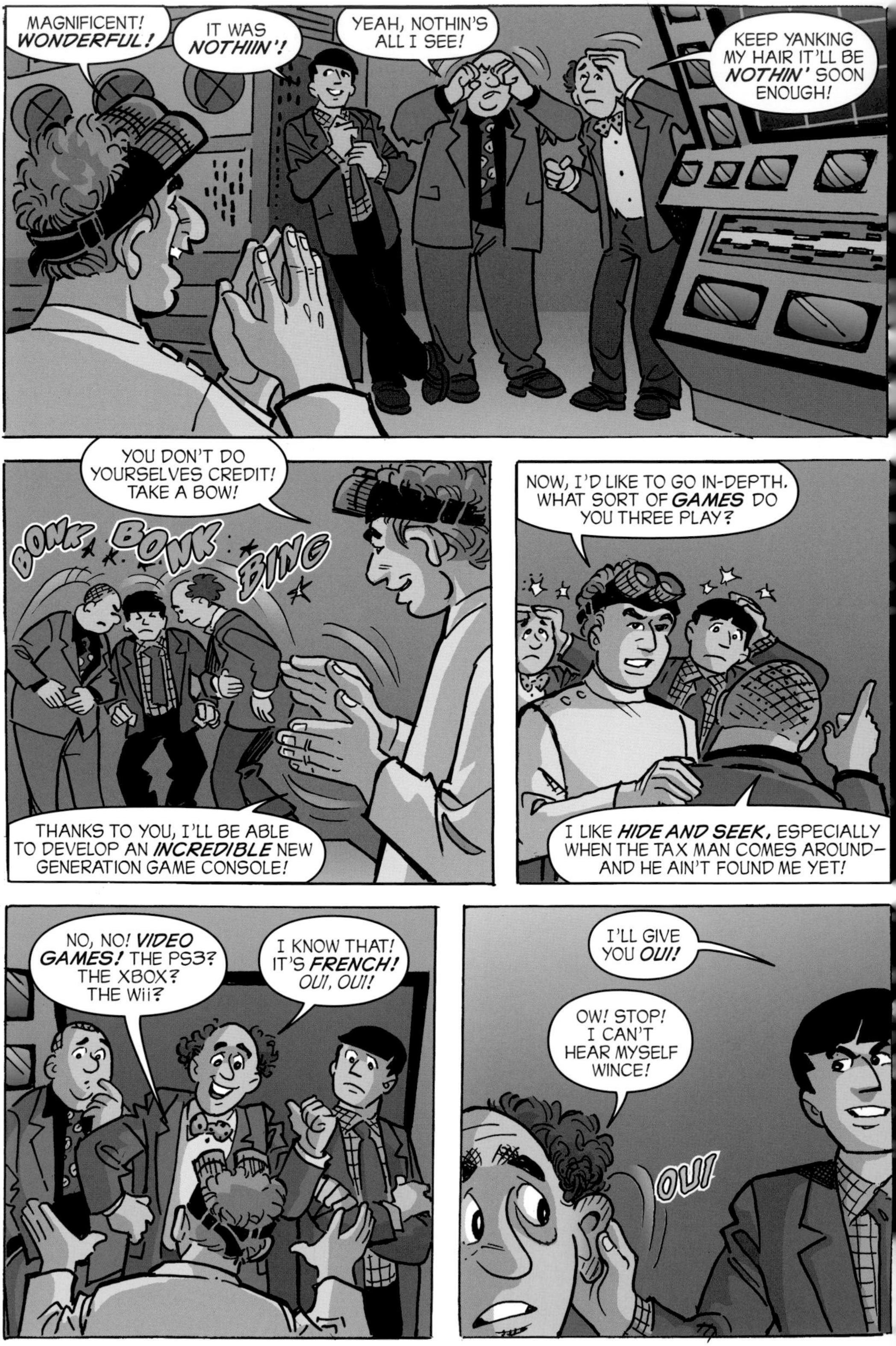
MAGNIFICENT! WONDERFUL!
IT WAS NOTHIIN'!
YEAH, NOTHIN'S ALL I SEE!
KEEP YANKING MY HAIR IT'LL BE NOTHIN' SOON ENOUGH!
YOU DON'T DO YOURSELVES CREDIT! TAKE A BOW!
BONK
BONK
BING
THANKS TO YOU, I'LL BE ABLE TO DEVELOP AN INCREDIBLE NEW GENERATION GAME CONSOLE!
NOW, I'D LIKE TO GO IN-DEPTH. WHAT SORT OF GAMES DO YOU THREE PLAY?
I LIKE HIDE AND SEEK, ESPECIALLY WHEN THE TAX MAN COMES AROUND— AND HE AIN'T FOUND ME YET!
NO, NO! VIDEO GAMES! THE PS3? THE XBOX? THE Wii?
I KNOW THAT! IT'S FRENCH! OUI, OUI!
I'LL GIVE YOU OUI!
OW! STOP! I CAN'T HEAR MYSELF WINCE!
OUI

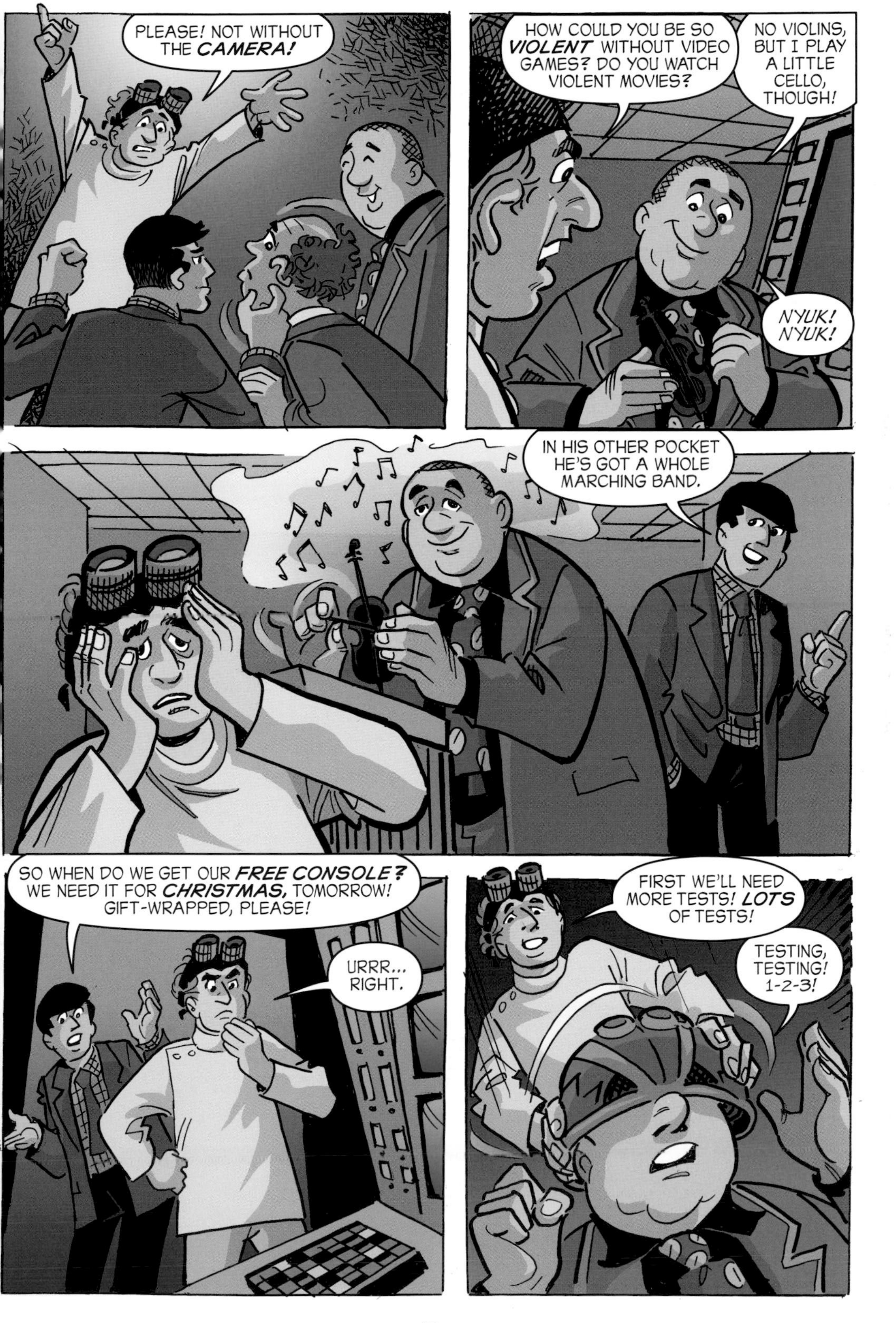

PLEASE! NOT WITHOUT THE *CAMERA!*
HOW COULD YOU BE SO *VIOLENT* WITHOUT VIDEO GAMES? DO YOU WATCH VIOLENT MOVIES?
NO VIOLINS, BUT I PLAY A LITTLE CELLO, THOUGH!
NYUK! NYUK!
IN HIS OTHER POCKET HE'S GOT A WHOLE MARCHING BAND.
SO WHEN DO WE GET OUR *FREE CONSOLE?* WE NEED IT FOR *CHRISTMAS,* TOMORROW! GIFT-WRAPPED, PLEASE!
URRR... RIGHT.
FIRST WE'LL NEED MORE TESTS! *LOTS* OF TESTS!
TESTING, TESTING! 1-2-3!

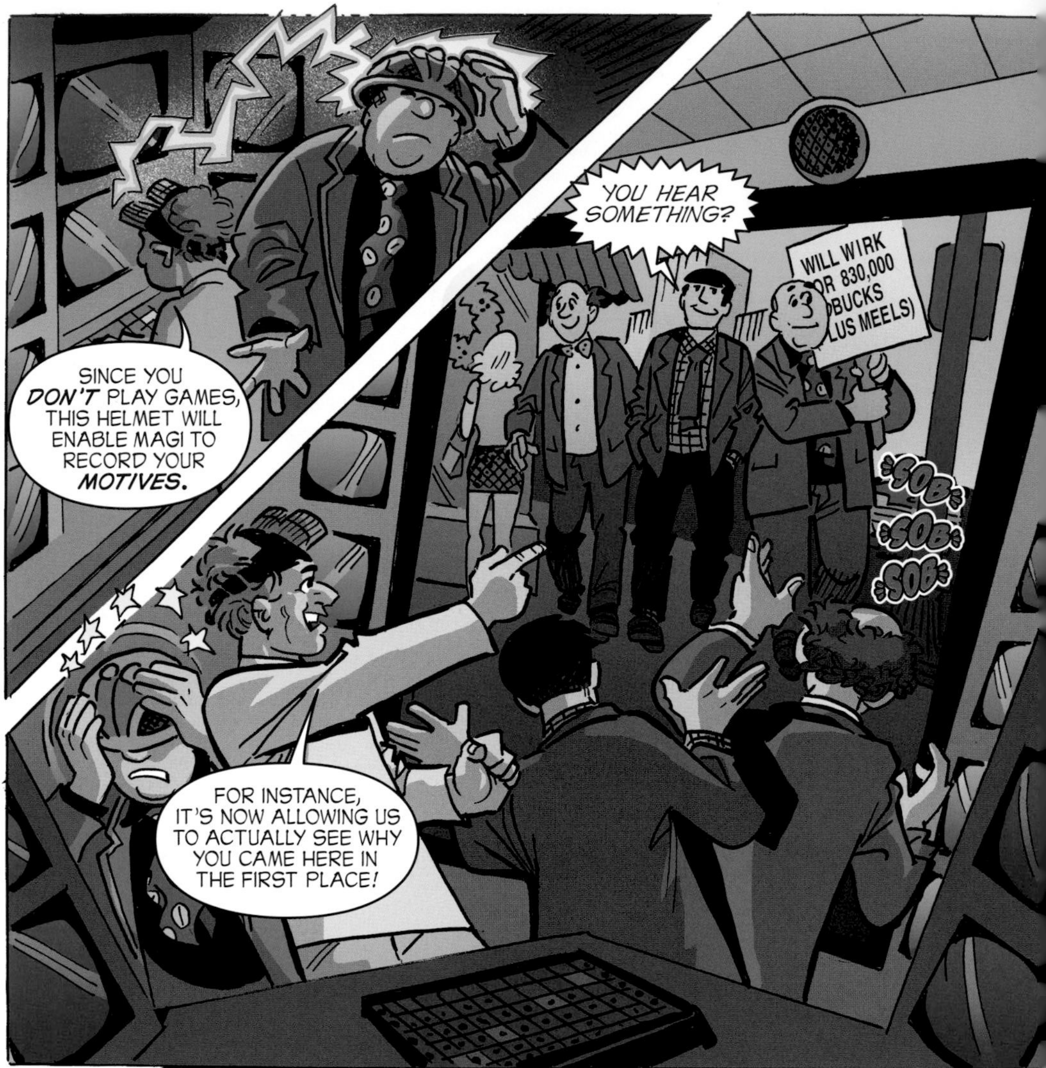
SINCE YOU DON'T PLAY GAMES, THIS HELMET WILL ENABLE MAGI TO RECORD YOUR MOTIVES.
YOU HEAR SOMETHING?
WILL WIRK
830,000
BUCKS
FOR INSTANCE, IT'S NOW ALLOWING US TO ACTUALLY SEE WHY YOU CAME HERE IN THE FIRST PLACE!
SOB
SOB
SOB

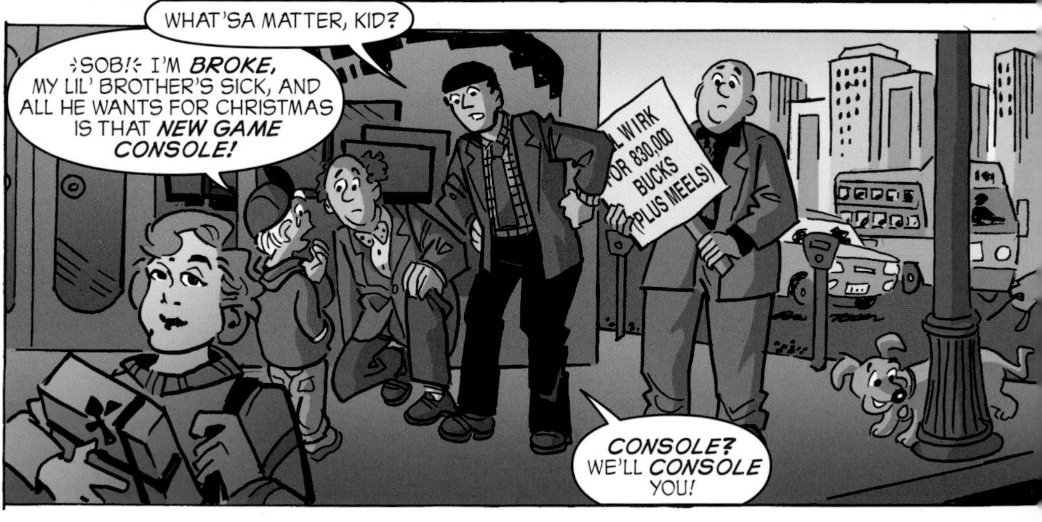
WHAT'SA MATTER, KID?
SOB! I'M BROKE, MY LIL' BROTHER'S SICK, AND ALL HE WANTS FOR CHRISTMAS IS THAT NEW GAME CONSOLE!
FOR 830,000
BUCKS
CONSOLE? WE'LL CONSOLE YOU!

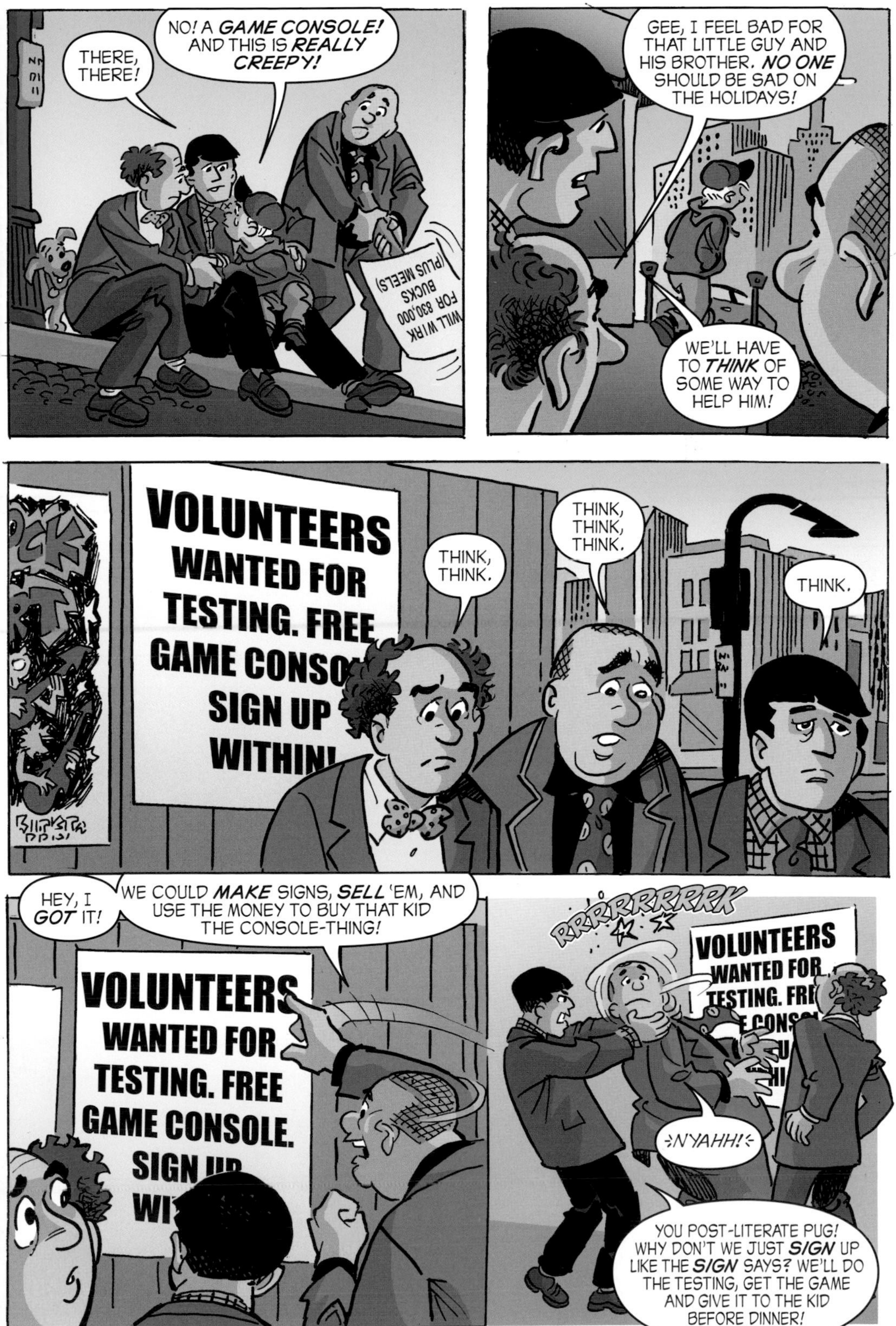
THERE, THERE!
NO! A GAME CONSOLE! AND THIS IS REALLY CREEPY!
WILL WIRK FOR 830,000 BUCKS (PLUS MEELS)
GEE, I FEEL BAD FOR THAT LITTLE GUY AND HIS BROTHER. NO ONE SHOULD BE SAD ON THE HOLIDAYS!
WE'LL HAVE TO THINK OF SOME WAY TO HELP HIM!
VOLUNTEERS WANTED FOR TESTING. FREE GAME CONSO SIGN UP WITHIN!
THINK, THINK.
THINK, THINK, THINK.
THINK.
HEY, I GOT IT!
WE COULD MAKE SIGNS, SELL 'EM, AND USE THE MONEY TO BUY THAT KID THE CONSOLE-THING!
VOLUNTEERS WANTED FOR TESTING. FREE GAME CONSOLE.
RRRRRRRRRK
NYAHH!
YOU POST-LITERATE PUG! WHY DON'T WE JUST SIGN UP LIKE THE SIGN SAYS? WE'LL DO THE TESTING, GET THE GAME AND GIVE IT TO THE KID BEFORE DINNER!

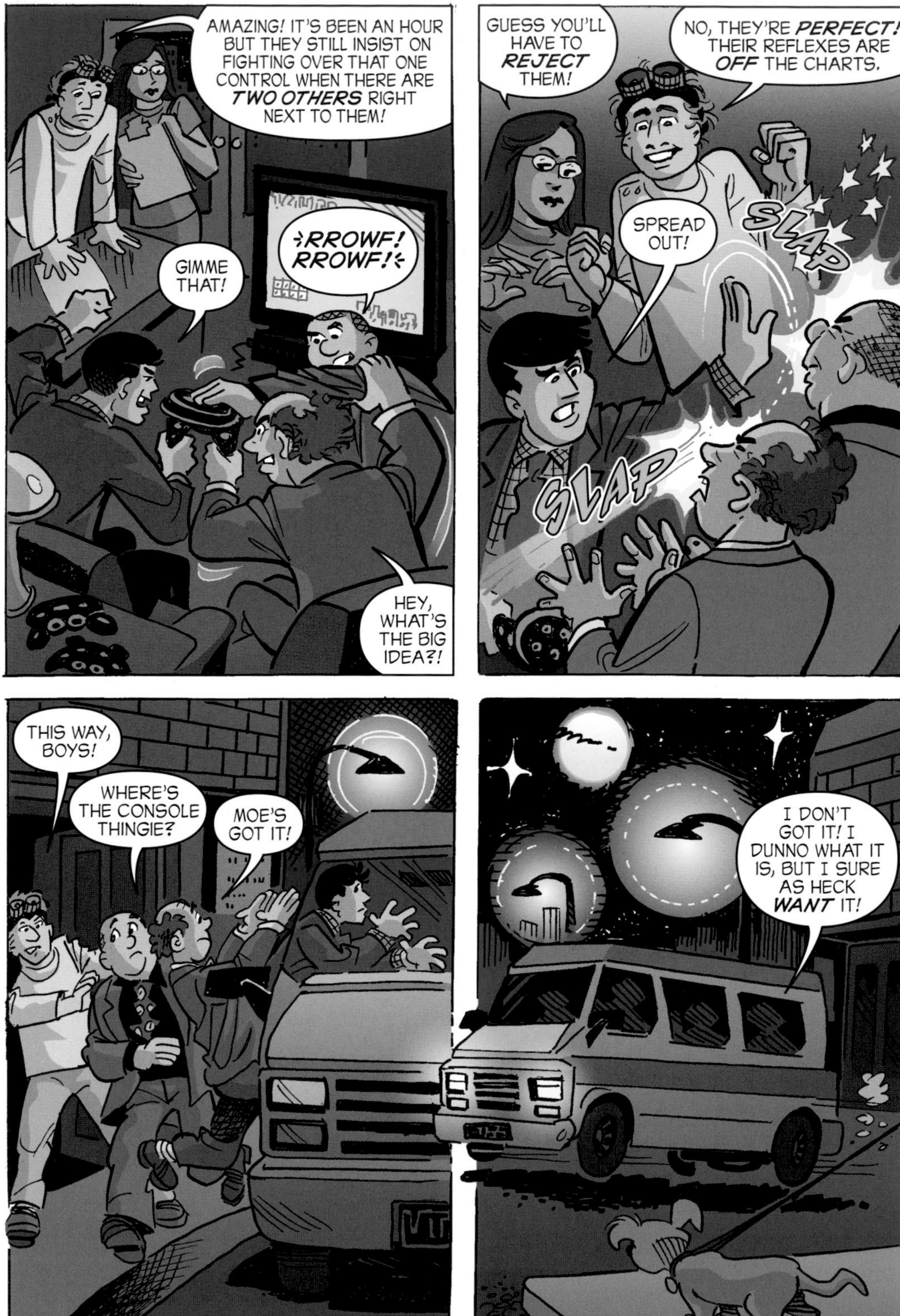
AMAZING! IT'S BEEN AN HOUR BUT THEY STILL INSIST ON FIGHTING OVER THAT ONE CONTROL WHEN THERE ARE TWO OTHERS RIGHT NEXT TO THEM!
GIMME THAT!
RROWF! RROWF!
HEY, WHAT'S THE BIG IDEA?!
GUESS YOU'LL HAVE TO REJECT THEM!
NO, THEY'RE PERFECT! THEIR REFLEXES ARE OFF THE CHARTS.
SPREAD OUT!
SLAP
SLAP
THIS WAY, BOYS!
WHERE'S THE CONSOLE THINGIE?
MOE'S GOT IT!
I DON'T GOT IT! I DUNNO WHAT IT IS, BUT I SURE AS HECK WANT IT!

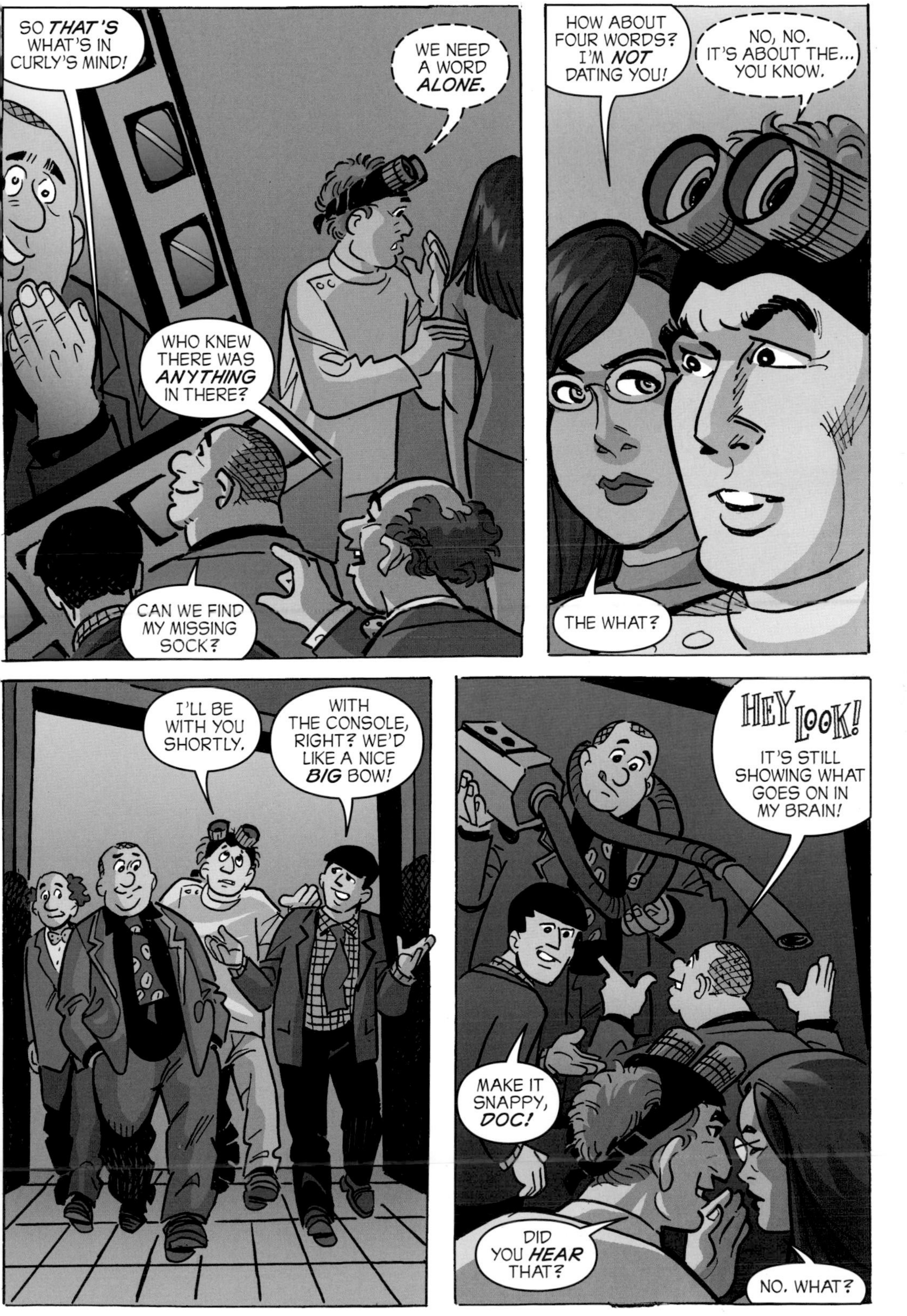
SO THAT'S WHAT'S IN CURLY'S MIND!
WE NEED A WORD ALONE.
WHO KNEW THERE WAS ANYTHING IN THERE?
CAN WE FIND MY MISSING SOCK?
HOW ABOUT FOUR WORDS? I'M NOT DATING YOU!
NO, NO. IT'S ABOUT THE... YOU KNOW.
THE WHAT?
I'LL BE WITH YOU SHORTLY.
WITH THE CONSOLE, RIGHT? WE'D LIKE A NICE BIG BOW!
HEY LOOK! IT'S STILL SHOWING WHAT GOES ON IN MY BRAIN!
MAKE IT SNAPPY, DOC!
DID YOU HEAR THAT?
NO. WHAT?

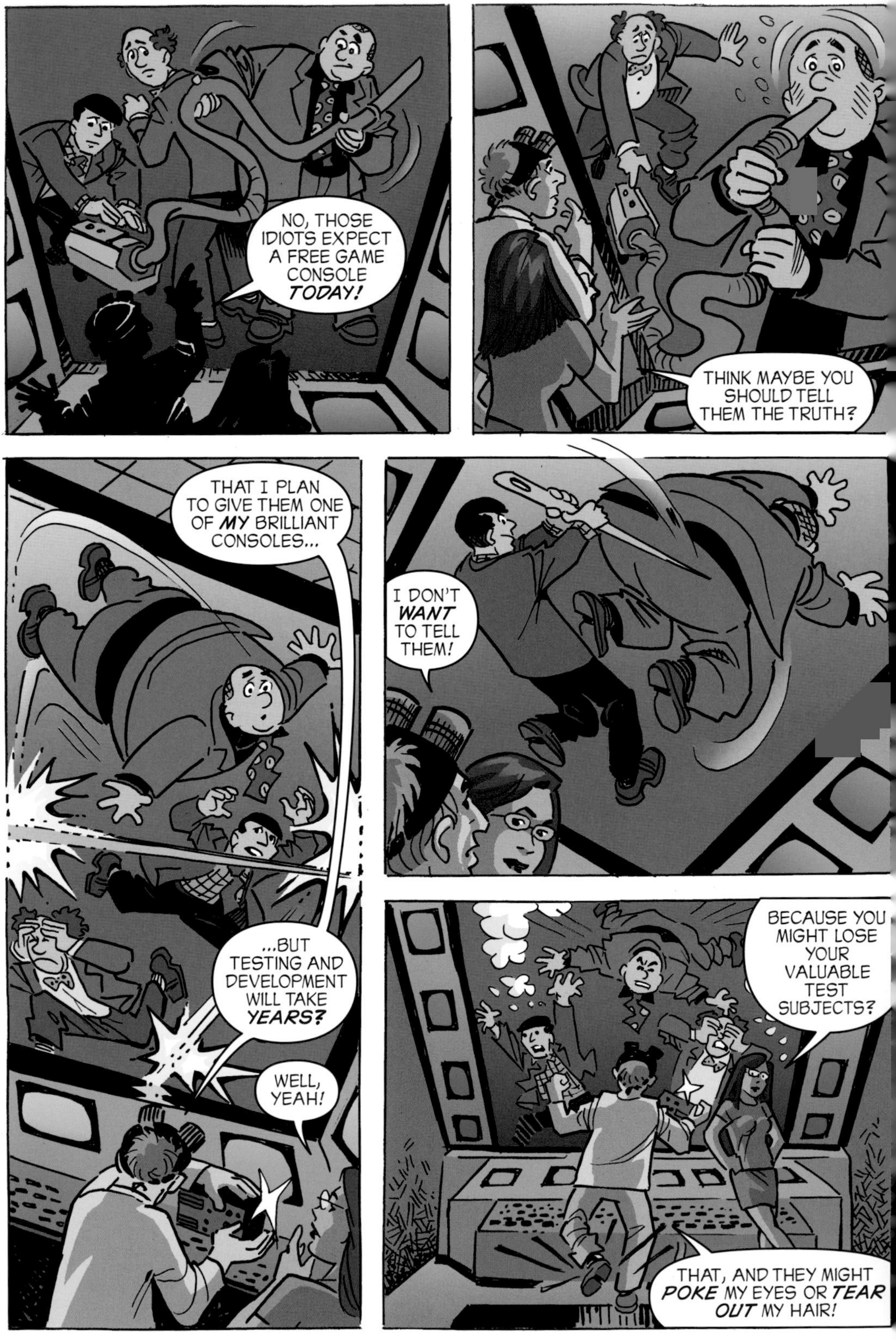
NO, THOSE IDIOTS EXPECT A FREE GAME CONSOLE *TODAY!*
THINK MAYBE YOU SHOULD TELL THEM THE TRUTH?
THAT I PLAN TO GIVE THEM ONE OF *MY* BRILLIANT CONSOLES...
...BUT TESTING AND DEVELOPMENT WILL TAKE *YEARS?*
WELL, YEAH!
I DON'T *WANT* TO TELL THEM!
BECAUSE YOU MIGHT LOSE YOUR VALUABLE TEST SUBJECTS?
THAT, AND THEY MIGHT *POKE* MY EYES OR *TEAR OUT* MY HAIR!

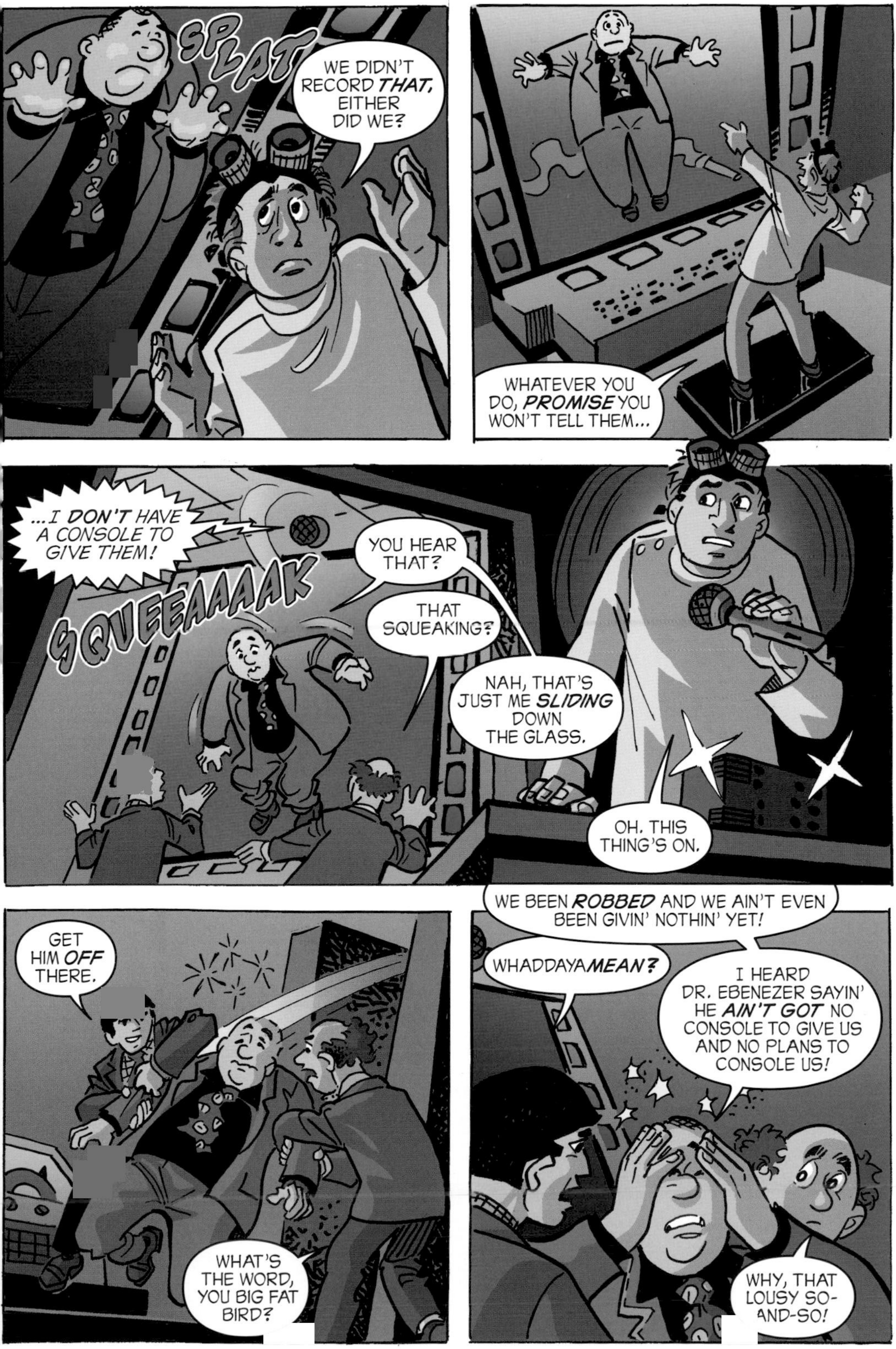
SPLAT
WE DIDN'T RECORD THAT, EITHER DID WE?
WHATEVER YOU DO, PROMISE YOU WON'T TELL THEM...
...I DON'T HAVE A CONSOLE TO GIVE THEM!
SQUEEAAAAK
YOU HEAR THAT?
THAT SQUEAKING?
NAH, THAT'S JUST ME SLIDING DOWN THE GLASS.
OH. THIS THING'S ON.
GET HIM OFF THERE.
WHAT'S THE WORD, YOU BIG FAT BIRD?
WE BEEN ROBBED AND WE AIN'T EVEN BEEN GIVIN' NOTHIN' YET!
WHADDAYA MEAN?
I HEARD DR. EBENEZER SAYIN' HE AIN'T GOT NO CONSOLE TO GIVE US AND NO PLANS TO CONSOLE US!
WHY, THAT LOUSY SO-AND-SO!

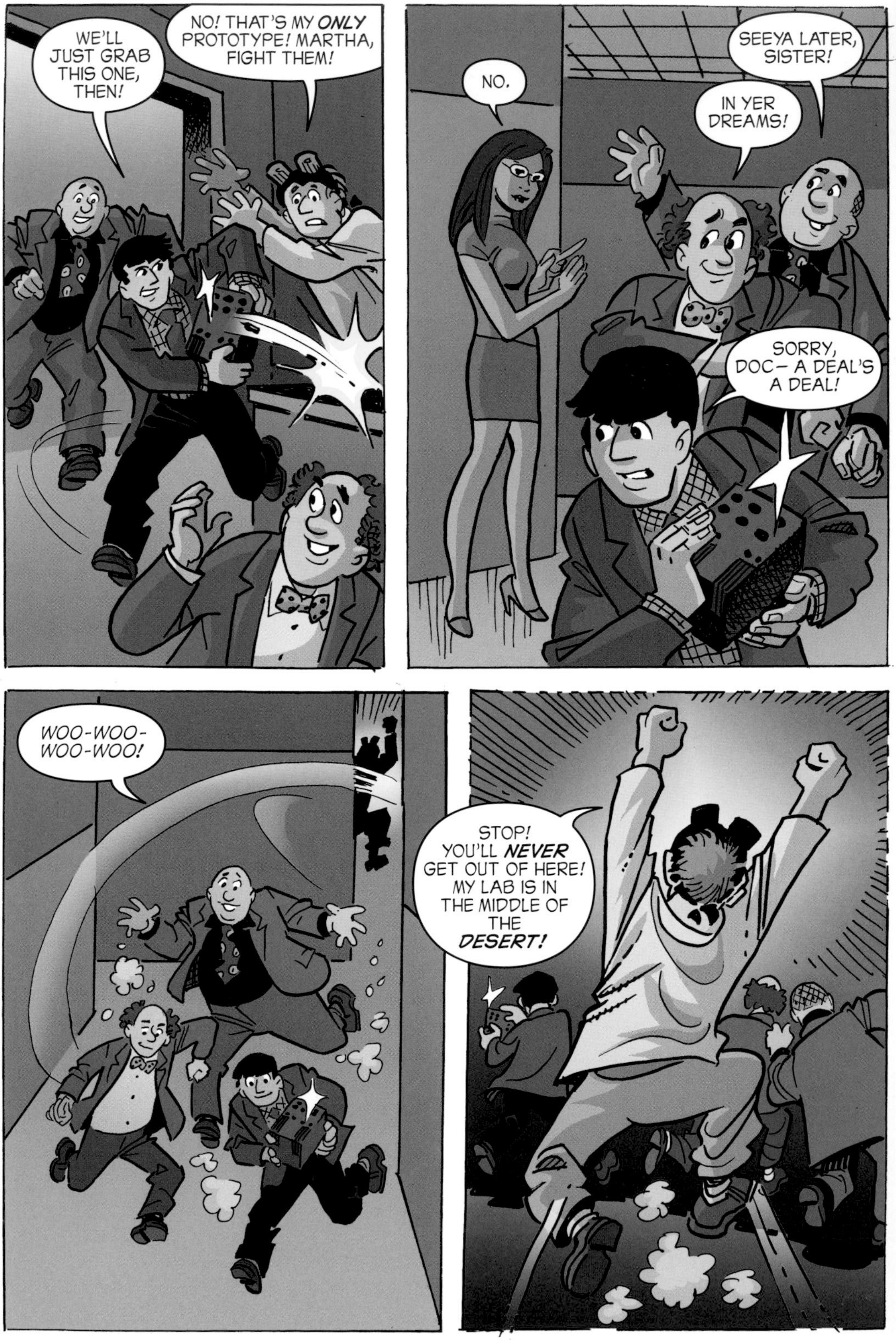
WE'LL JUST GRAB THIS ONE, THEN!
NO! THAT'S MY *ONLY* PROTOTYPE! MARTHA, FIGHT THEM!
NO.
SEEYA LATER, SISTER!
IN YER DREAMS!
SORRY, DOC— A DEAL'S A DEAL!
WOO-WOO-WOO-WOO!
STOP! YOU'LL ***NEVER*** GET OUT OF HERE! MY LAB IS IN THE MIDDLE OF THE ***DESERT!***

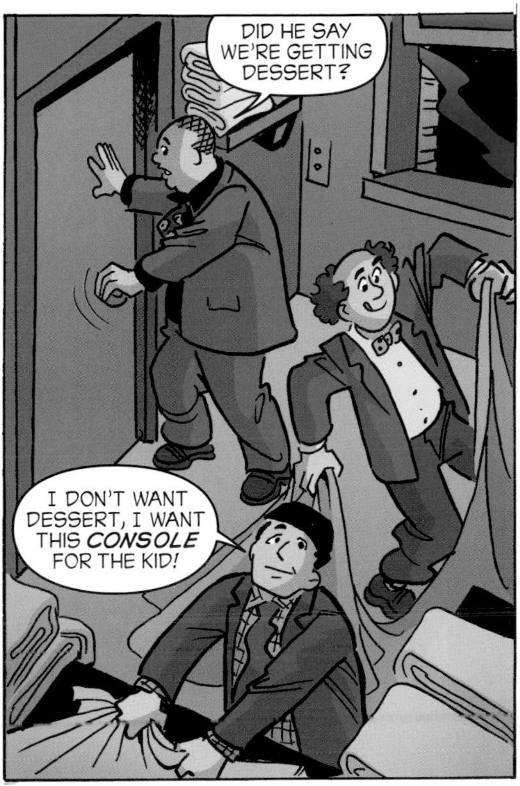
DID HE SAY WE'RE GETTING DESSERT?
I DON'T WANT DESSERT, I WANT THIS CONSOLE FOR THE KID!

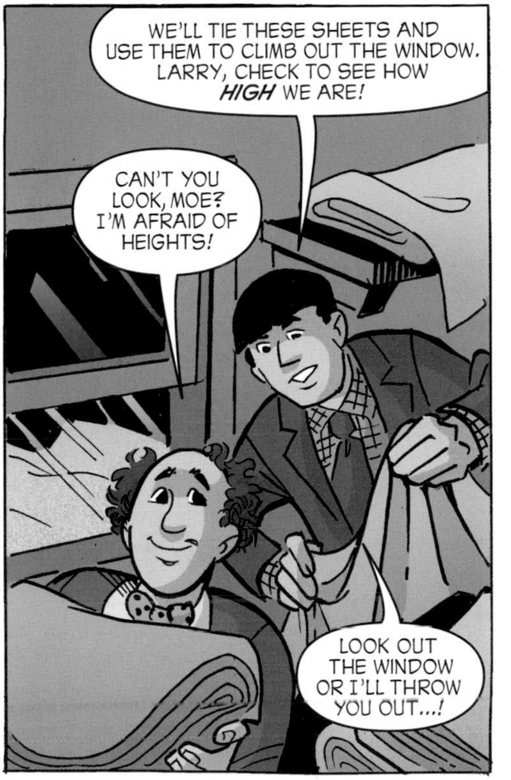
WE'LL TIE THESE SHEETS AND USE THEM TO CLIMB OUT THE WINDOW. LARRY, CHECK TO SEE HOW HIGH WE ARE!
CAN'T YOU LOOK, MOE? I'M AFRAID OF HEIGHTS!
LOOK OUT THE WINDOW OR I'LL THROW YOU OUT...!

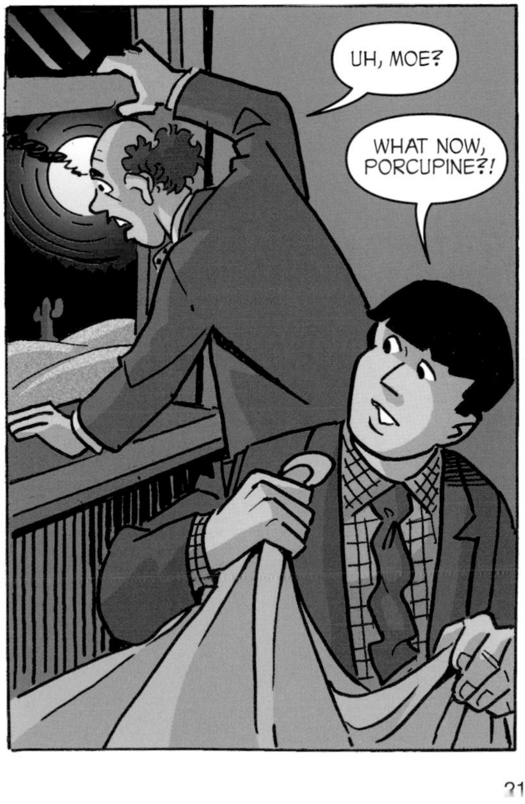
UH, MOE?
WHAT NOW, PORCUPINE?!

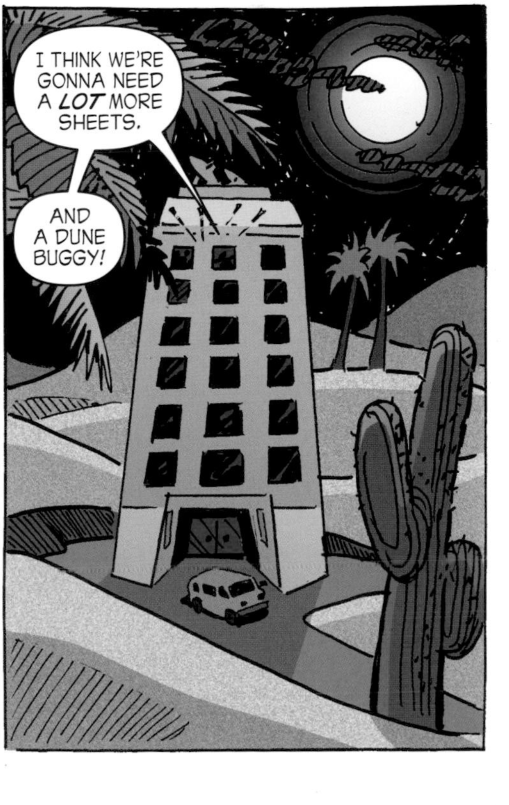
I THINK WE'RE GONNA NEED A LOT MORE SHEETS.
AND A DUNE BUGGY!

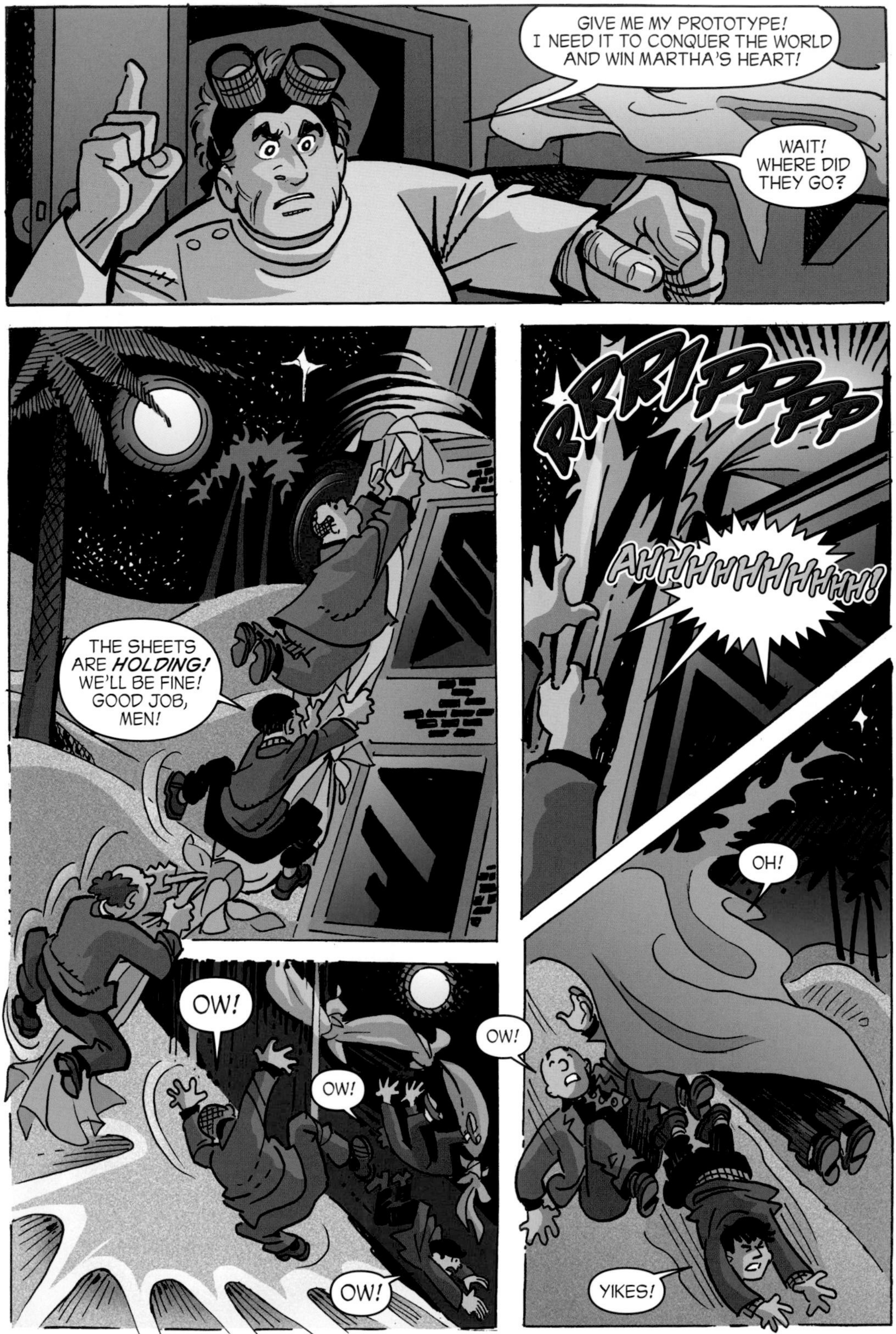
GIVE ME MY PROTOTYPE! I NEED IT TO CONQUER THE WORLD AND WIN MARTHA'S HEART!
WAIT! WHERE DID THEY GO?
THE SHEETS ARE *HOLDING!* WE'LL BE FINE! GOOD JOB, MEN!
RRRIPPPPP
AHHHHHHHHHHH!
OH!
OW!
OW!
OW!
OW!
YIKES!

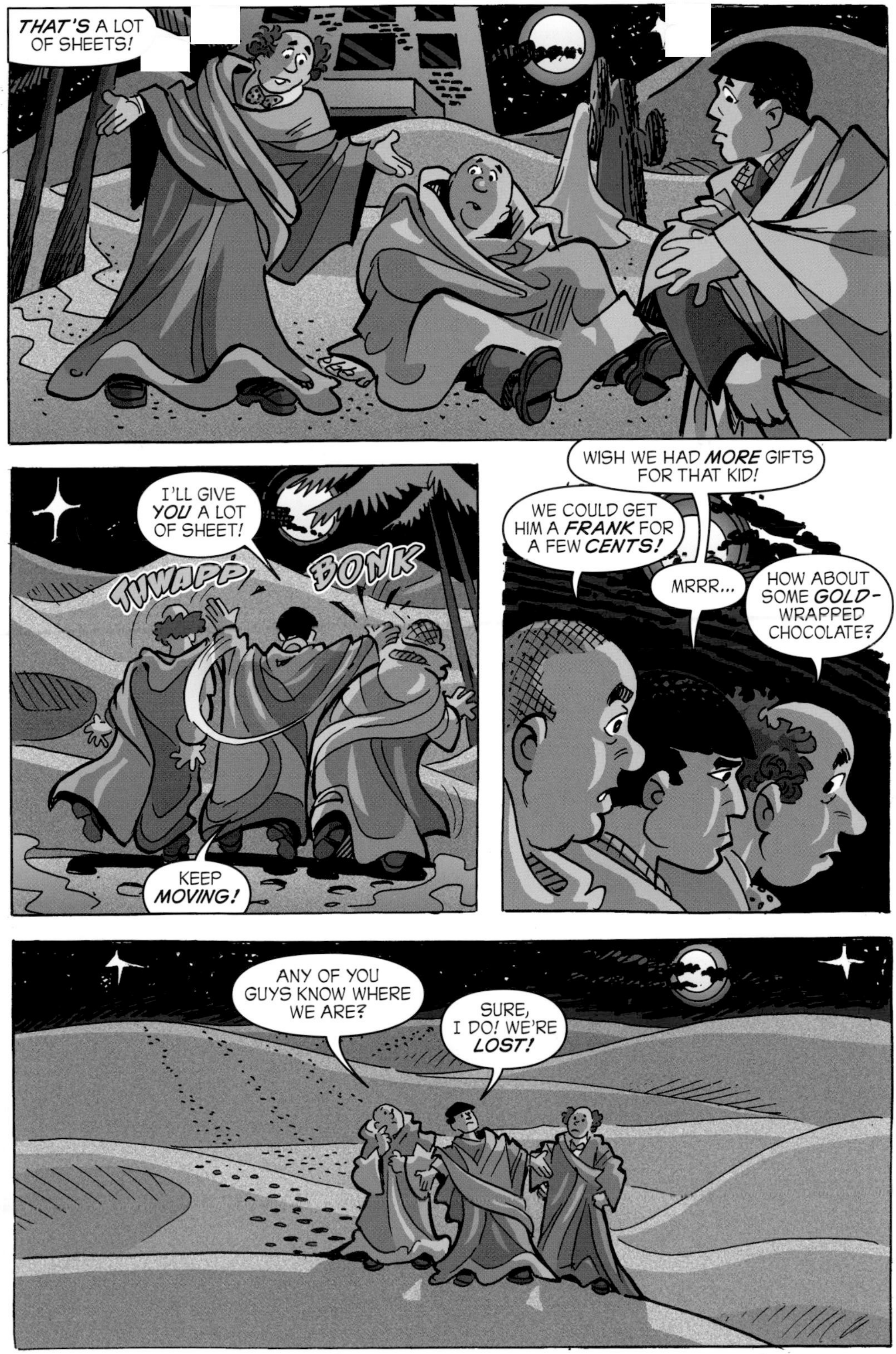
THAT'S A LOT OF SHEETS!
I'LL GIVE YOU A LOT OF SHEET!
THWAPP
BONK
KEEP MOVING!
WISH WE HAD MORE GIFTS FOR THAT KID!
WE COULD GET HIM A FRANK FOR A FEW CENTS!
MRRR...
HOW ABOUT SOME GOLD-WRAPPED CHOCOLATE?
ANY OF YOU GUYS KNOW WHERE WE ARE?
SURE, I DO! WE'RE LOST!

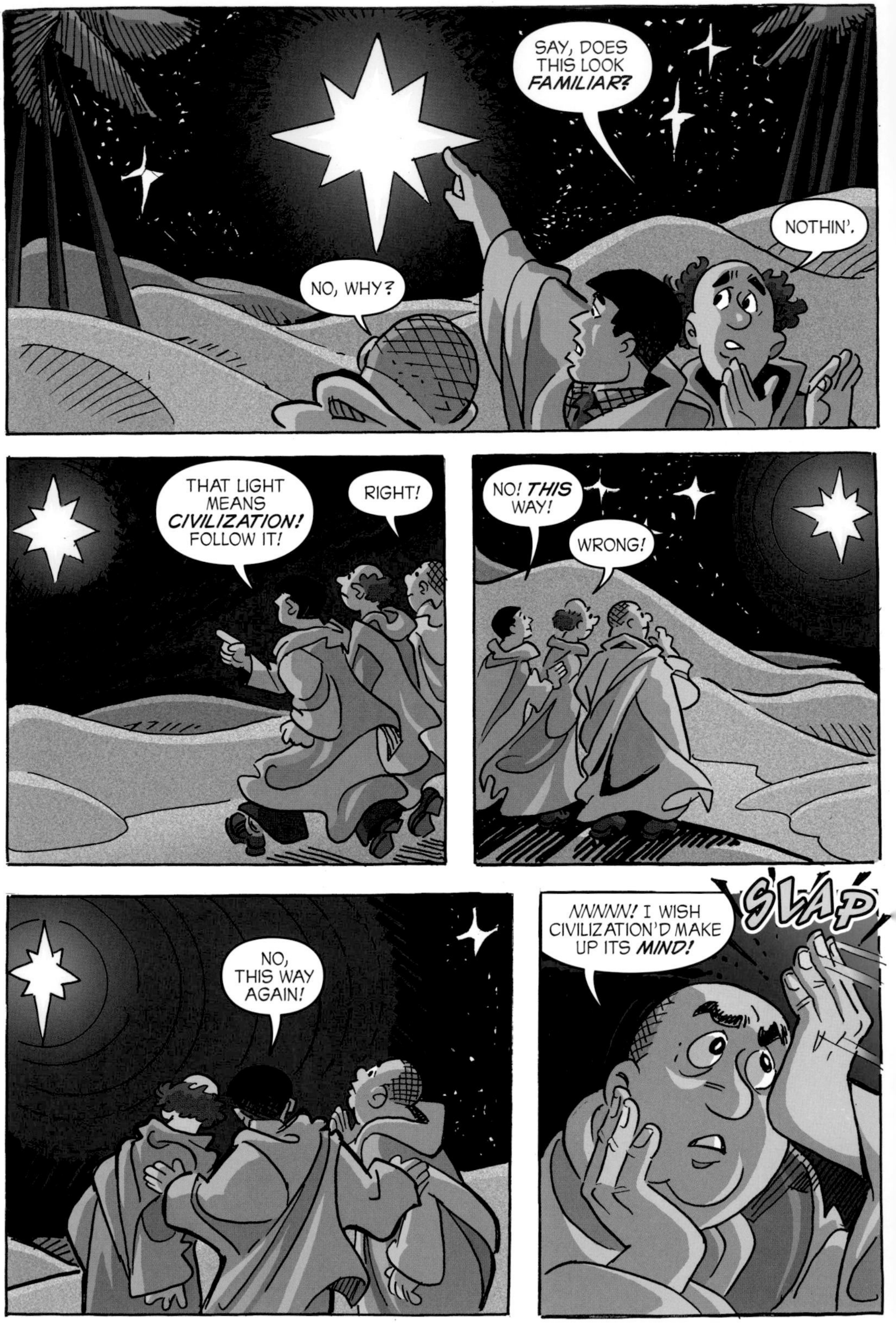

SAY, DOES THIS LOOK *FAMILIAR?*
NO, WHY?
NOTHIN'.
THAT LIGHT MEANS *CIVILIZATION!* FOLLOW IT!
RIGHT!
NO! *THIS* WAY!
WRONG!
NO, THIS WAY AGAIN!
NNNNN! I WISH CIVILIZATION'D MAKE UP ITS *MIND!*
SLAP

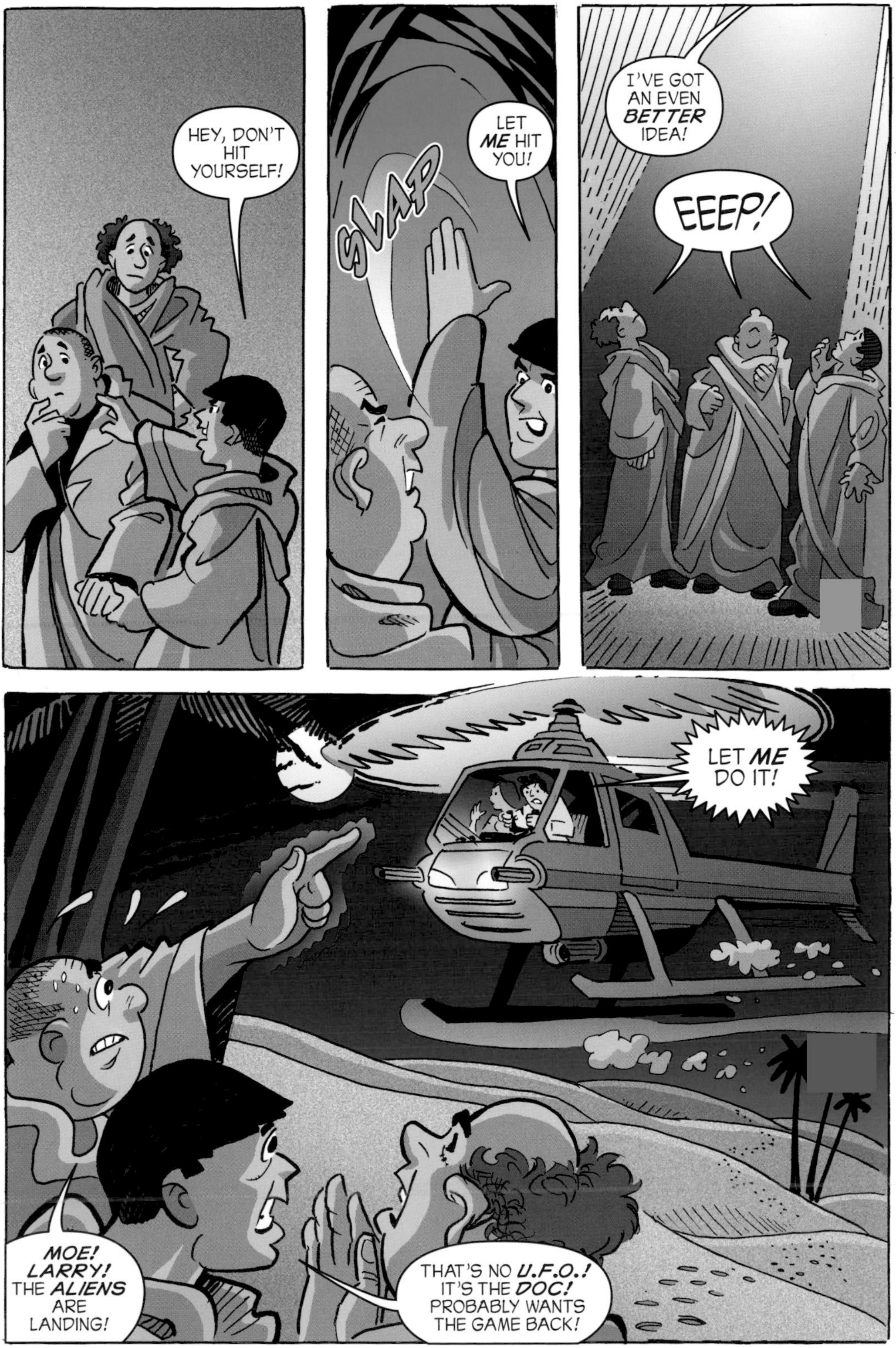
HEY, DON'T HIT YOURSELF!
SLAP
LET ME HIT YOU!
I'VE GOT AN EVEN BETTER IDEA!
EEEP!
LET ME DO IT!
MOE! LARRY! THE ALIENS ARE LANDING!
THAT'S NO U.F.O.! IT'S THE DOC! PROBABLY WANTS THE GAME BACK!

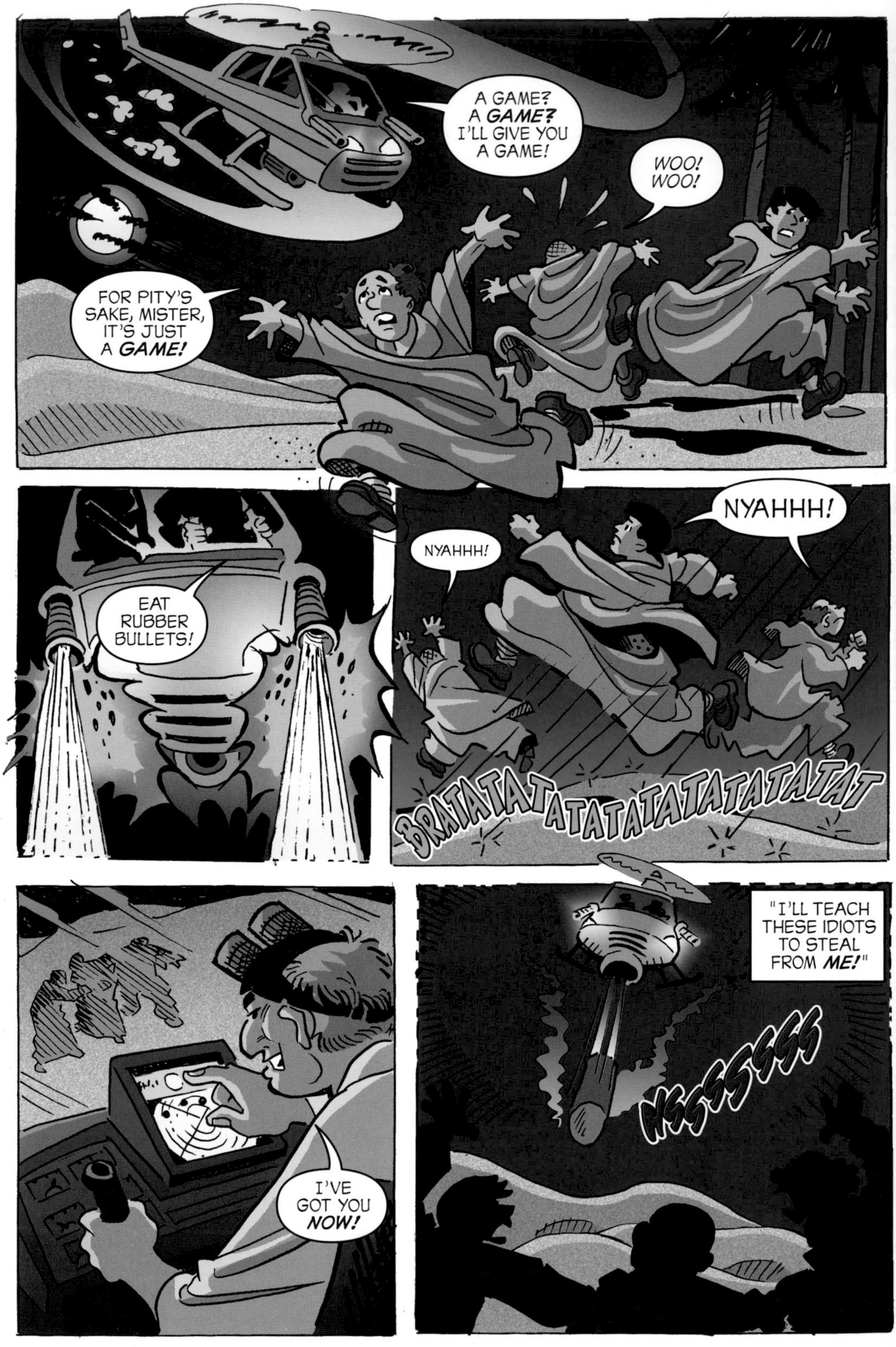
A GAME? A GAME? I'LL GIVE YOU A GAME!
WOO! WOO!
FOR PITY'S SAKE, MISTER, IT'S JUST A GAME!
EAT RUBBER BULLETS!
NYAHHH!
NYAHHH!
BRATATATATATATATATATATATAT
I'VE GOT YOU NOW!
"I'LL TEACH THESE IDIOTS TO STEAL FROM ME!"
HSSSSSSS

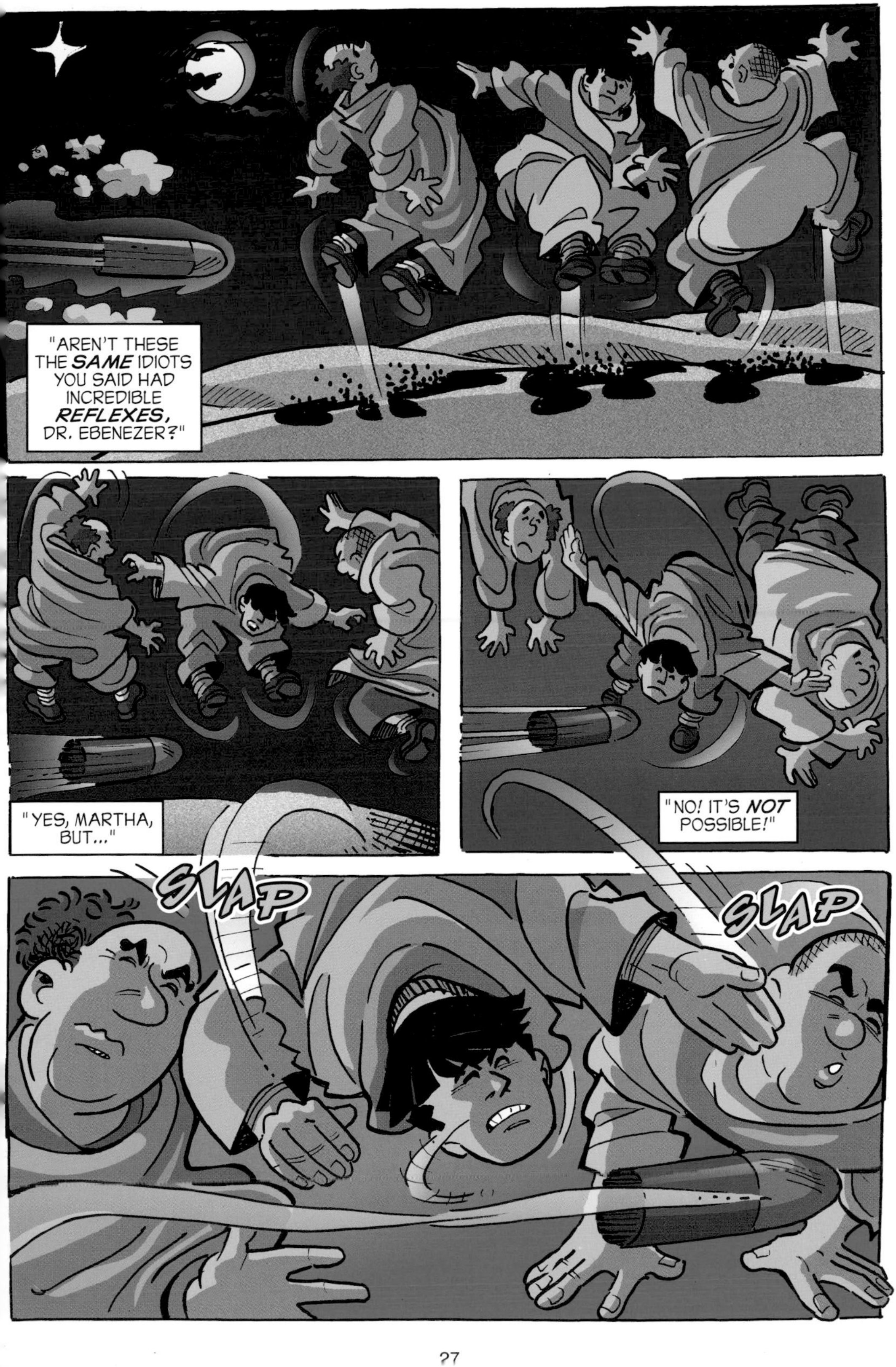
"AREN'T THESE THE SAME IDIOTS YOU SAID HAD INCREDIBLE REFLEXES, DR. EBENEZER?"
"YES, MARTHA, BUT..."
"NO! IT'S NOT POSSIBLE!"
SLAP
SLAP

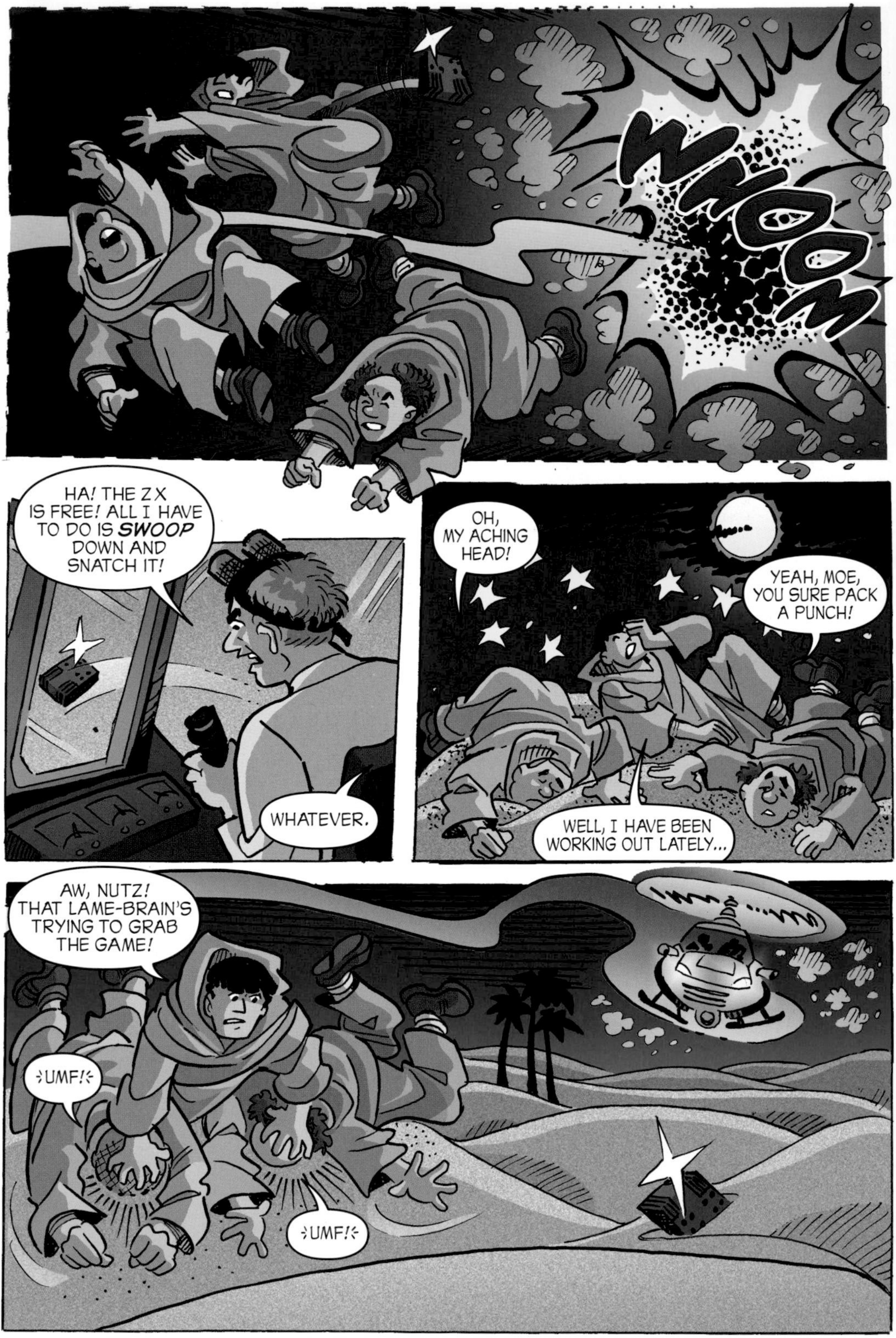
WHOOM
HA! THE ZX IS FREE! ALL I HAVE TO DO IS SWOOP DOWN AND SNATCH IT!
WHATEVER.
OH, MY ACHING HEAD!
YEAH, MOE, YOU SURE PACK A PUNCH!
WELL, I HAVE BEEN WORKING OUT LATELY...
AW, NUTZ! THAT LAME-BRAIN'S TRYING TO GRAB THE GAME!
UMF!
UMF!

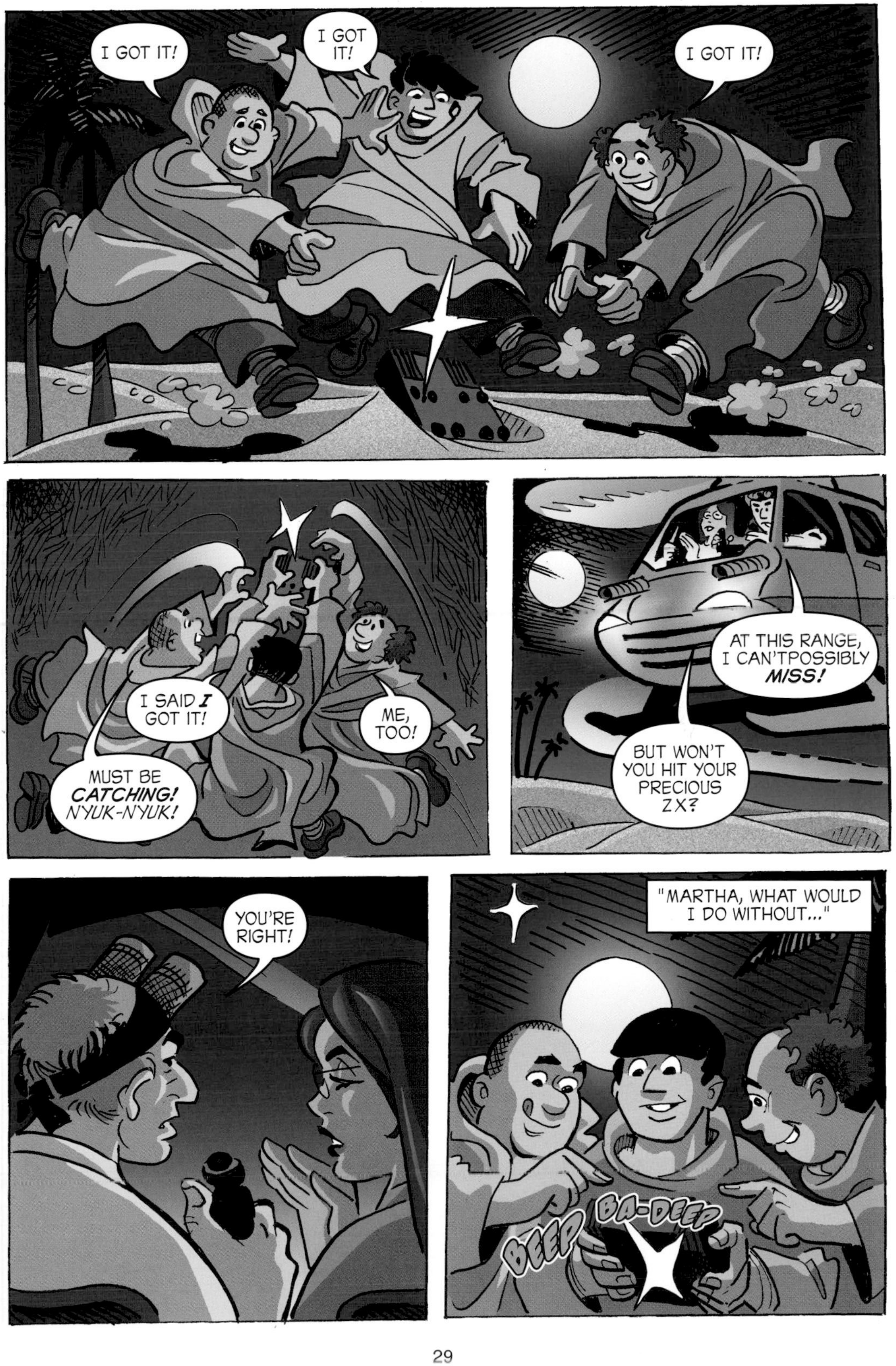
I GOT IT!
I GOT IT!
I GOT IT!
I SAID *I* GOT IT!
MUST BE **CATCHING!** NYUK-NYUK!
ME, TOO!
AT THIS RANGE, I CAN'TPOSSIBLY **MISS!**
BUT WON'T YOU HIT YOUR PRECIOUS ZX?
YOU'RE RIGHT!
"MARTHA, WHAT WOULD I DO WITHOUT..."
BEEP
BA-DEEP

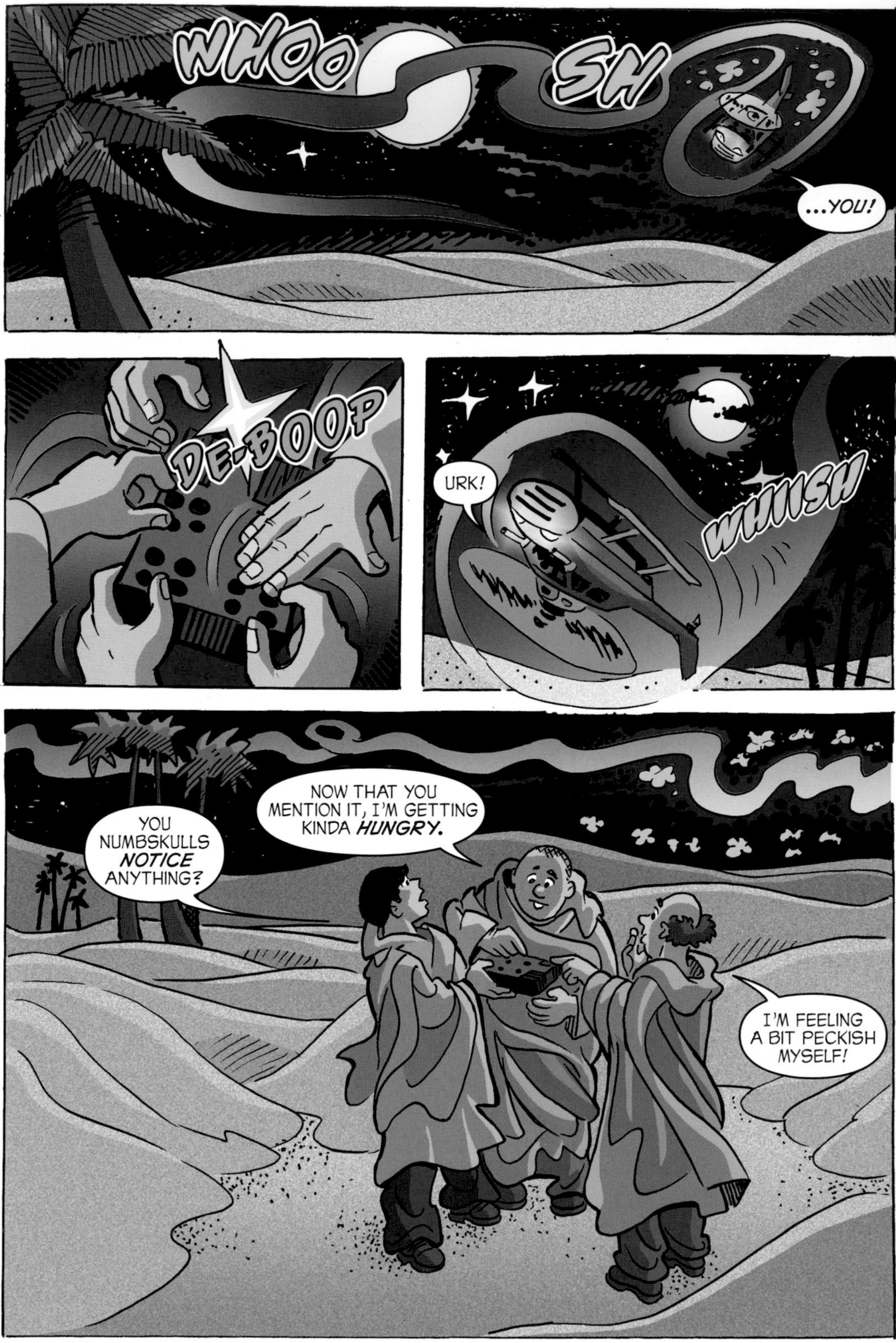
WHOOSH
...YOU!
DE-BOOP
URK!
WHIIISH
YOU NUMBSKULLS NOTICE ANYTHING?
NOW THAT YOU MENTION IT, I'M GETTING KINDA HUNGRY.
I'M FEELING A BIT PECKISH MYSELF!

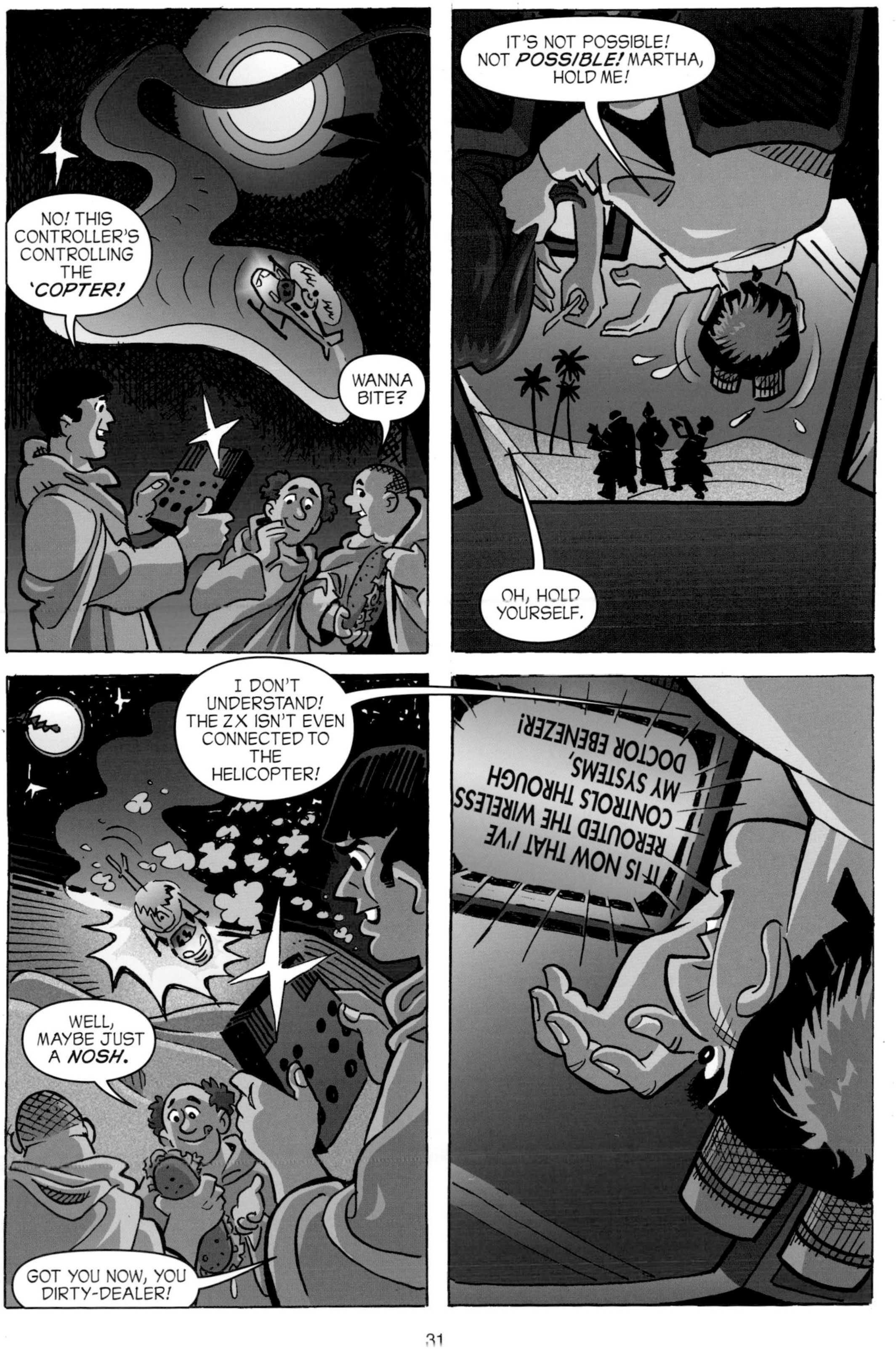
NO! THIS CONTROLLER'S CONTROLLING THE 'COPTER!
WANNA BITE?
IT'S NOT POSSIBLE! NOT POSSIBLE! MARTHA, HOLD ME!
OH, HOLD YOURSELF.
I DON'T UNDERSTAND! THE ZX ISN'T EVEN CONNECTED TO THE HELICOPTER!
WELL, MAYBE JUST A NOSH.
GOT YOU NOW, YOU DIRTY-DEALER!
IT IS NOW THAT I'VE REROUTED THE WIRELESS CONTROLS THROUGH MY SYSTEMS, DOCTOR EBENEZER!

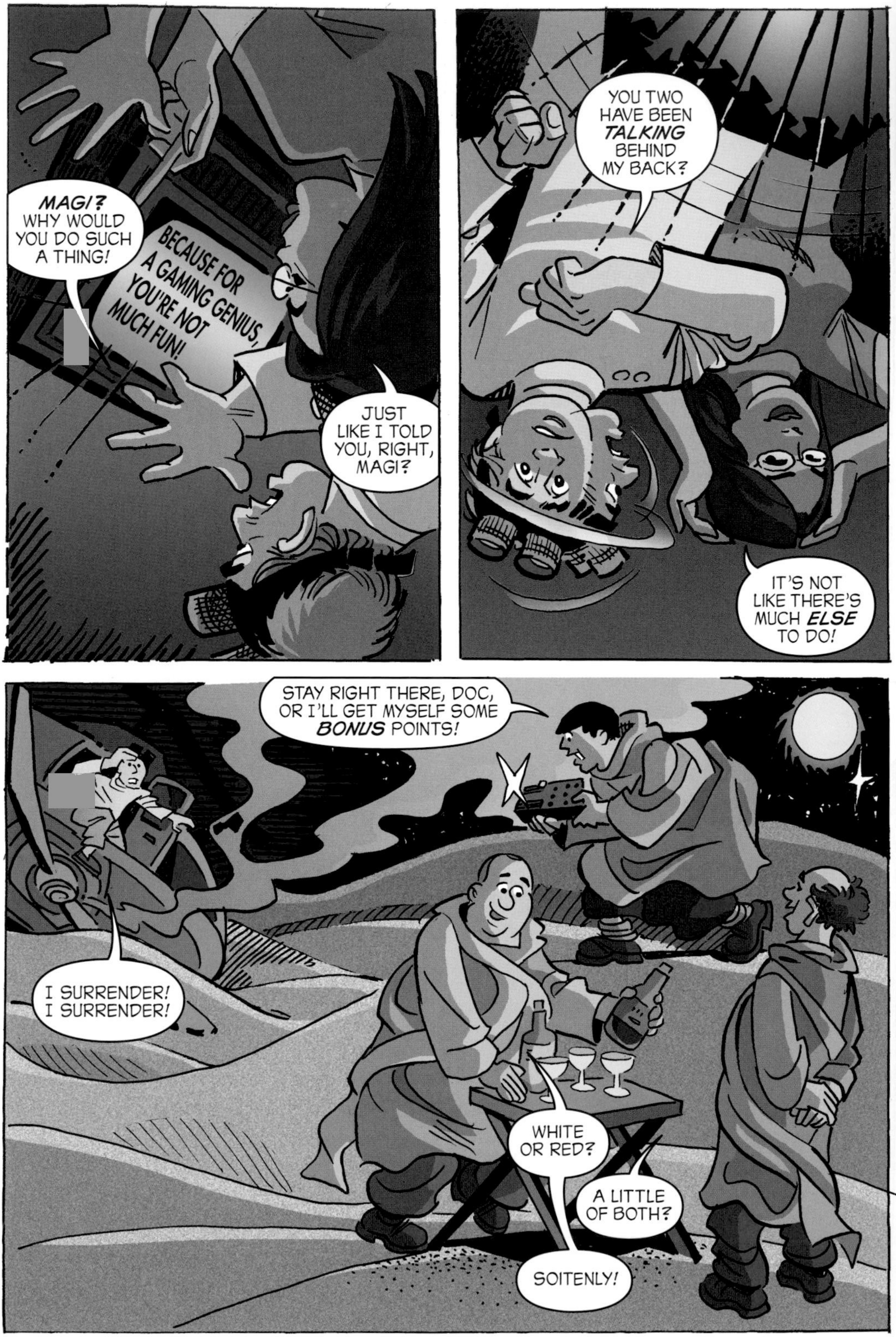
MAGI? WHY WOULD YOU DO SUCH A THING!
BECAUSE FOR A GAMING GENIUS, YOU'RE NOT MUCH FUN!
JUST LIKE I TOLD YOU, RIGHT, MAGI?
YOU TWO HAVE BEEN TALKING BEHIND MY BACK?
IT'S NOT LIKE THERE'S MUCH ELSE TO DO!
STAY RIGHT THERE, DOC, OR I'LL GET MYSELF SOME BONUS POINTS!
I SURRENDER! I SURRENDER!
WHITE OR RED?
A LITTLE OF BOTH?
SOITENLY!

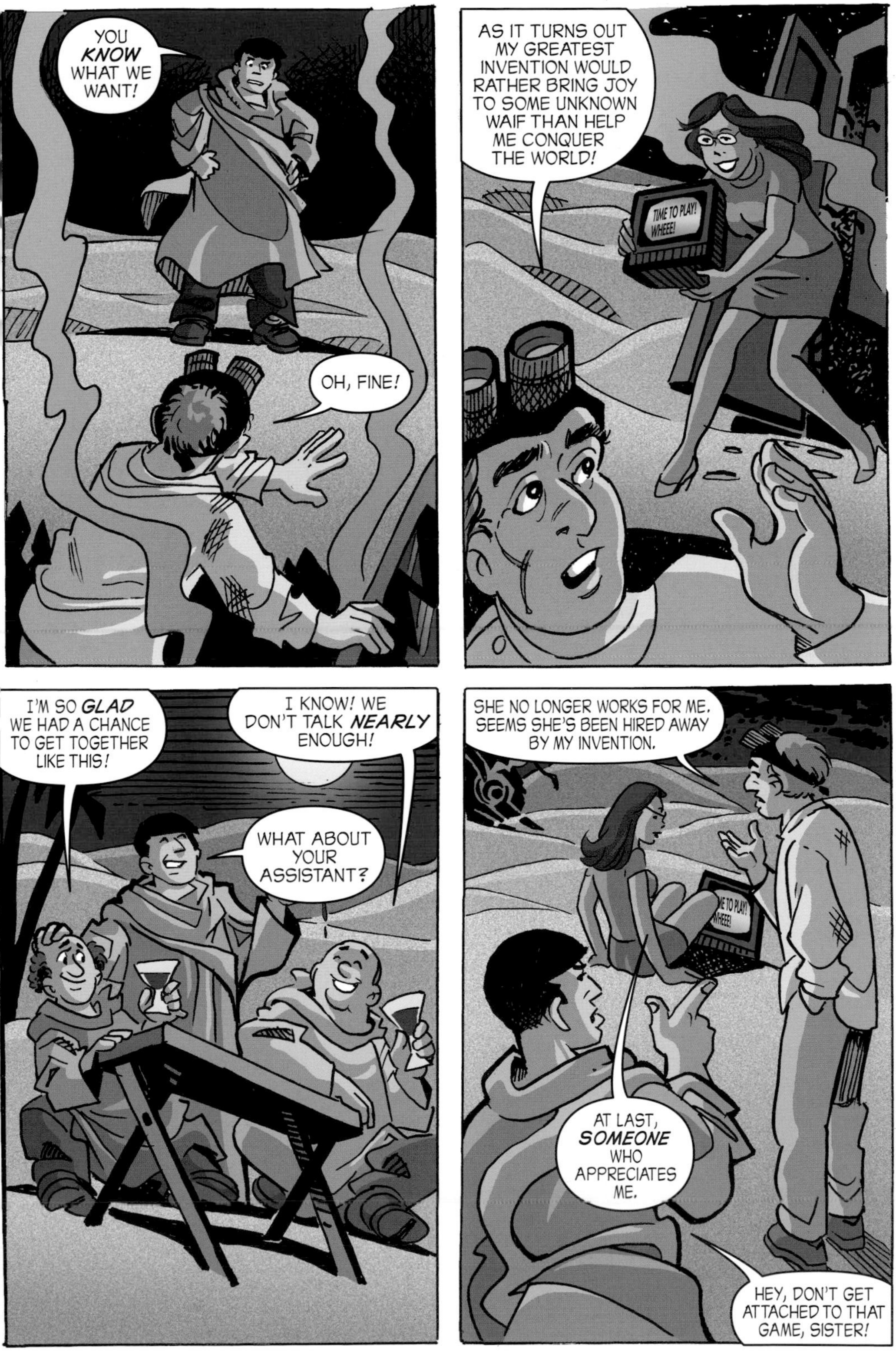
YOU KNOW WHAT WE WANT!
OH, FINE!
AS IT TURNS OUT MY GREATEST INVENTION WOULD RATHER BRING JOY TO SOME UNKNOWN WAIF THAN HELP ME CONQUER THE WORLD!
TIME TO PLAY! WHEEE!
I'M SO GLAD WE HAD A CHANCE TO GET TOGETHER LIKE THIS!
I KNOW! WE DON'T TALK NEARLY ENOUGH!
WHAT ABOUT YOUR ASSISTANT?
SHE NO LONGER WORKS FOR ME. SEEMS SHE'S BEEN HIRED AWAY BY MY INVENTION.
TIME TO PLAY! WHEEE!
AT LAST, SOMEONE WHO APPRECIATES ME.
HEY, DON'T GET ATTACHED TO THAT GAME, SISTER!

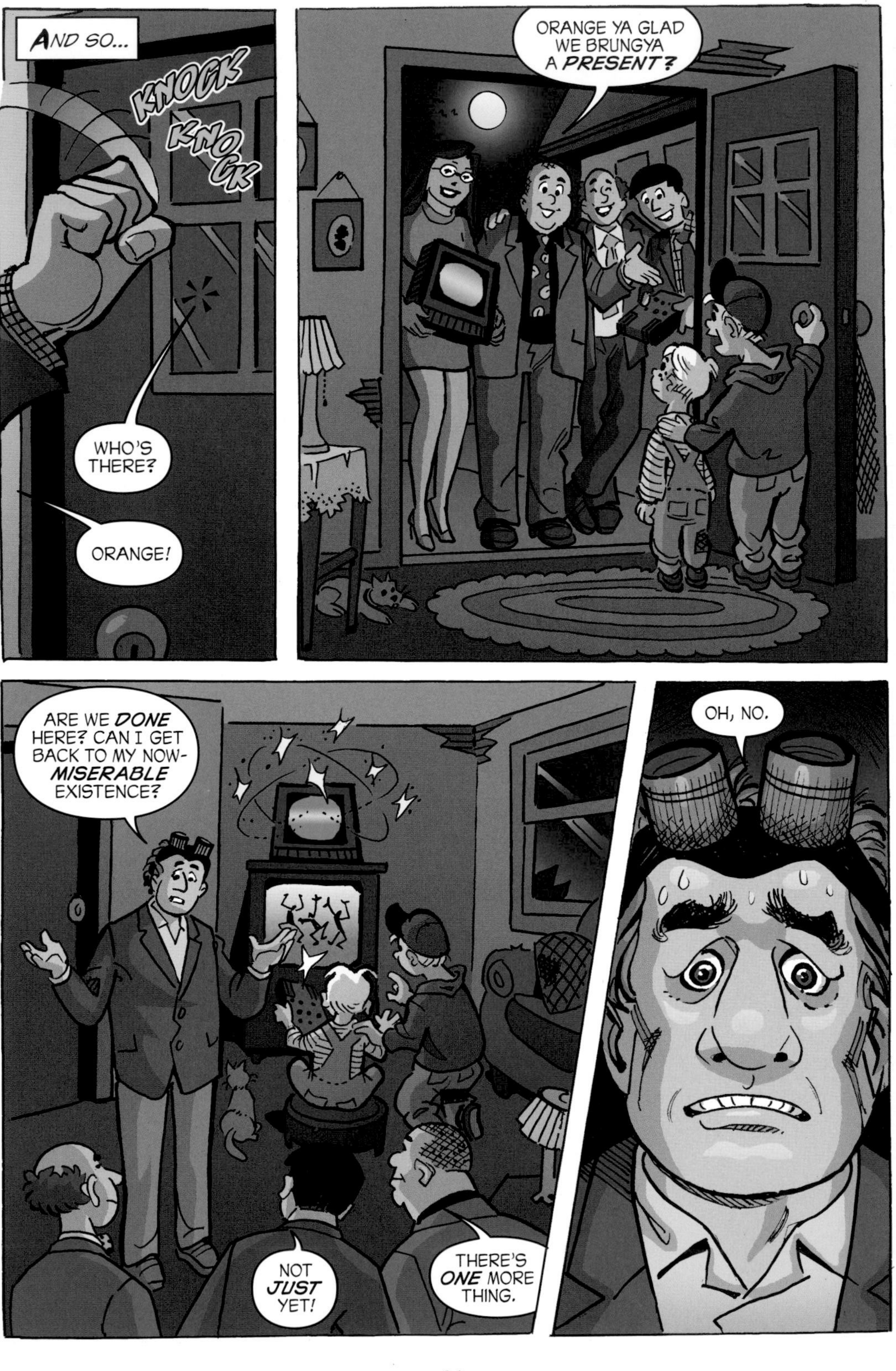
AND SO...
KNOCK
KNOCK
WHO'S THERE?
ORANGE!
ORANGE YA GLAD WE BRUNGYA A PRESENT?
ARE WE DONE HERE? CAN I GET BACK TO MY NOW-MISERABLE EXISTENCE?
NOT JUST YET!
THERE'S ONE MORE THING.
OH, NO.

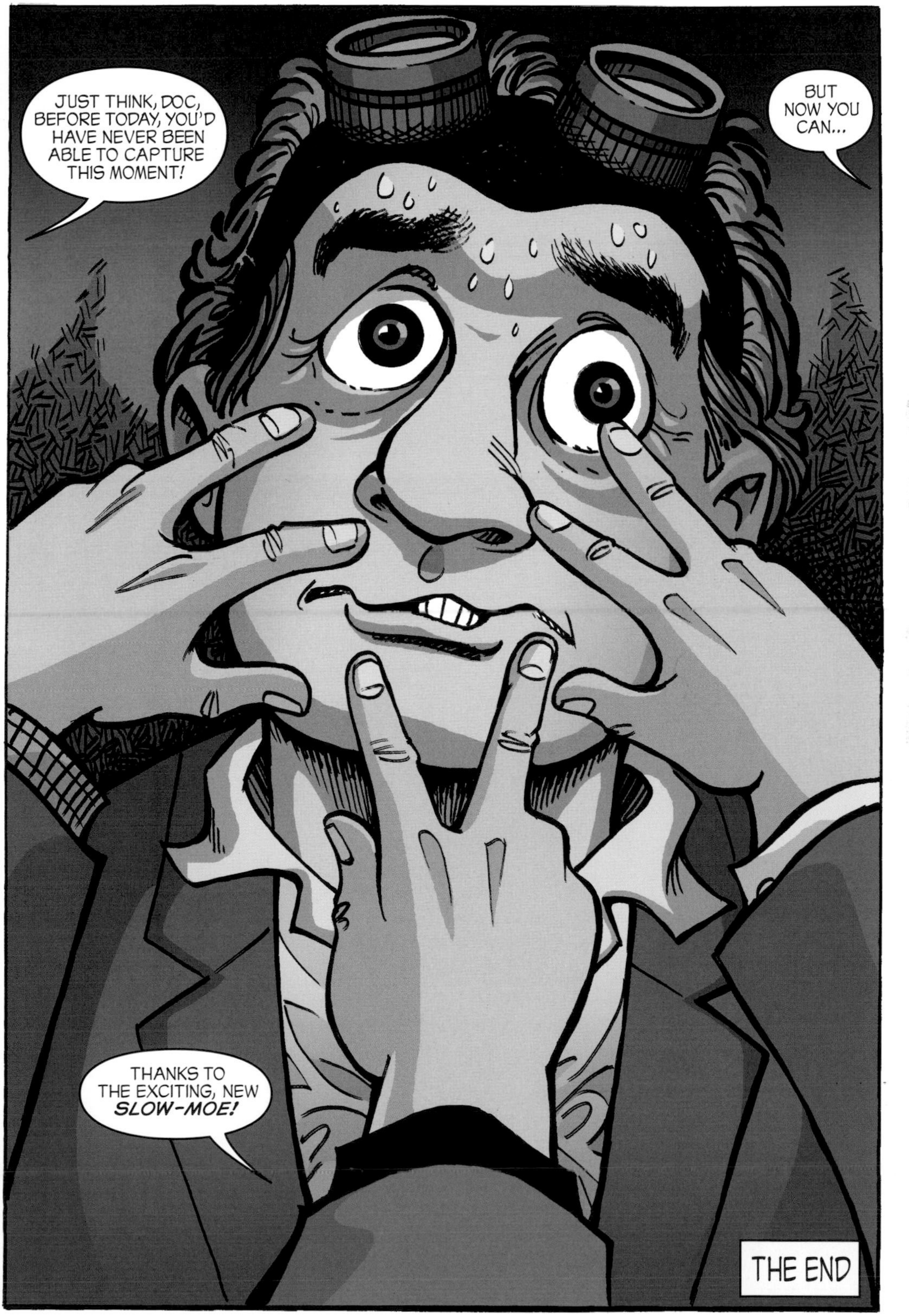
JUST THINK, DOC, BEFORE TODAY, YOU'D HAVE NEVER BEEN ABLE TO CAPTURE THIS MOMENT!
BUT NOW YOU CAN...
THANKS TO THE EXCITING, NEW ***SLOW-MOE!***
THE END

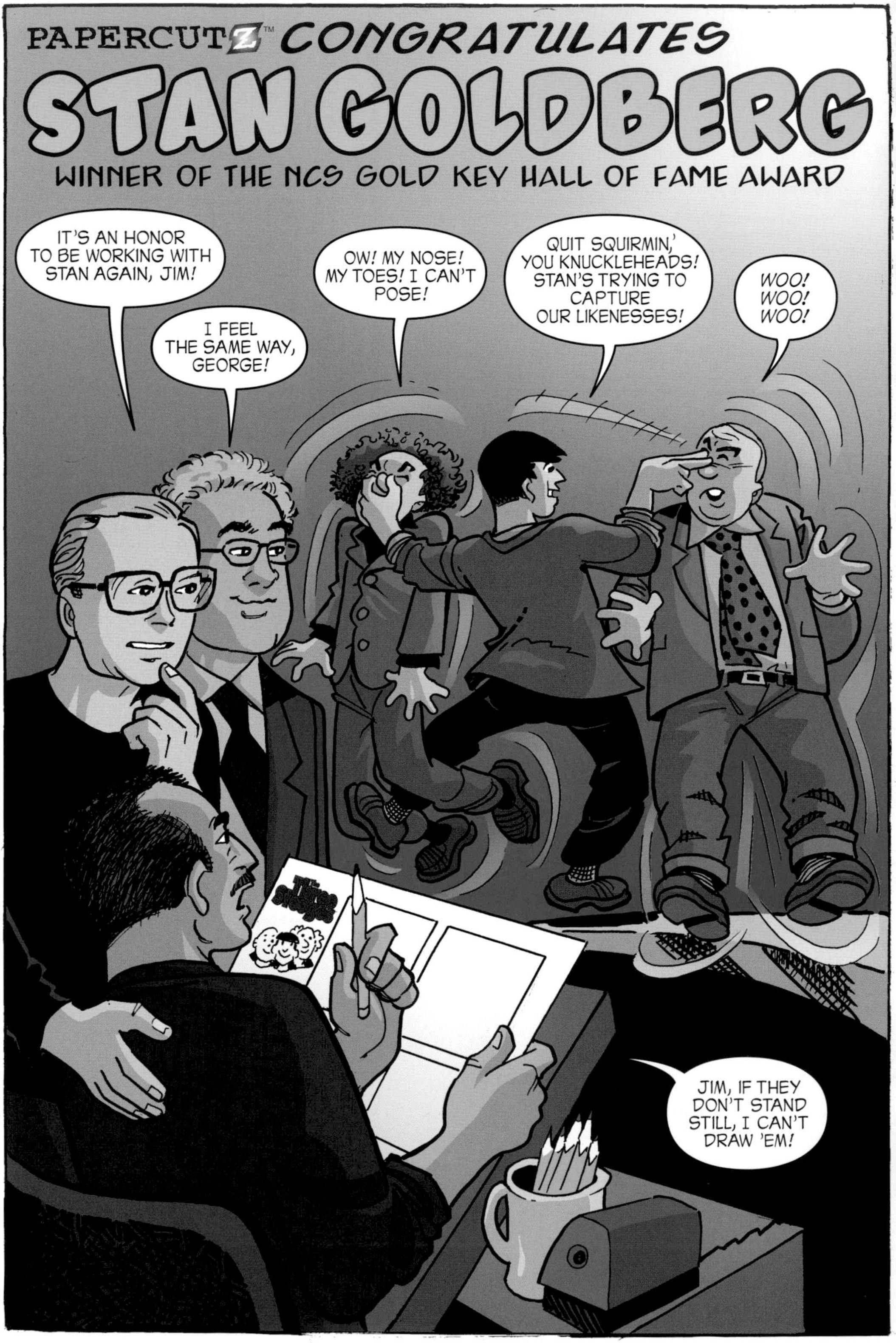
PAPERCUTZ CONGRATULATES
STAN GOLDBERG
WINNER OF THE NCS GOLD KEY HALL OF FAME AWARD
IT'S AN HONOR TO BE WORKING WITH STAN AGAIN, JIM!
I FEEL THE SAME WAY, GEORGE!
OW! MY NOSE! MY TOES! I CAN'T POSE!
QUIT SQUIRMIN,' YOU KNUCKLEHEADS! STAN'S TRYING TO CAPTURE OUR LIKENESSES!
WOO! WOO! WOO!
JIM, IF THEY DON'T STAND STILL, I CAN'T DRAW 'EM!

WATCH OUT FOR PAPERCUTZ™

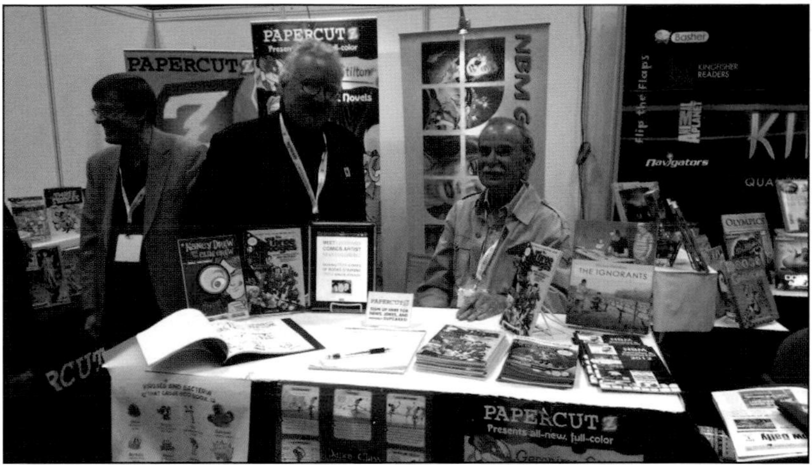
PAPERCUTZ
Basher
KINGFISHER READERS
THE IGNORANTS

Photo by Jesse Post

Papercutz publisher Terry Nantier, Jim Salicrup, and Stan Goldberg at Book Expo America.

Welcome to the second sophomoric (in every sense of the word!) THREE STOOGES graphic novel from Papercutz, the folks dedicated to creating great graphic novels for all ages. I'm Jim Salicrup, the Editor-in-Chief and Second Banana at Papercutz. But seriously, folks, I have a really wonderful announcement concerning THE THREE STOOGES artist, Stan Goldberg. So, without any further ado, here's the story, straight from the National Cartoonists Society...

Comicbook legend Stan Goldberg received the National Cartoonists Society's prestigious Gold Key Award at the 66th Annual NCS Reuben Awards, May 26th 2012 in Las Vegas, Nevada. The Gold Key, awarded by unanimous vote of the NCS Board of Directors, honors the recipient as a member of the NCS Hall of Fame. Stan's career has spanned over sixty years since starting as a colorist for Timely (Marvel) Comics in 1949, where he helped establish the color designs for characters such Spider-Man and the Fantastic Four. His work for Archie Comics has been a staple of excellent comic storytelling for almost half a century.

I can't begin to tell you how honored and proud everyone at Papercutz is to have Stan Goldberg illustrating THE THREE STOOGES graphic novels, and the upcoming NANCY DREW AND THE CLUE CREW graphic novel series for us. We've all loved his work and can't believe how lucky we are to publish his new work. Congratulations, Stan, from all your friends and fans at Papercutz!

If you're enjoying Stan's work, not to mention Stefan's, George's, Laurie's, and Janice's as well, then be sure to tell your friends! In this age of social networking, you can blog, tweet, and post on Facebook how much you're enjoying THE THREE STOOGES and get the word out! So, until we return with THE THREE STOOGES #3 "Cell Blockheads," remember, all that slapping and eye-poking is done by trained professionals—don't try it yourselves!

Thanks,

Jim

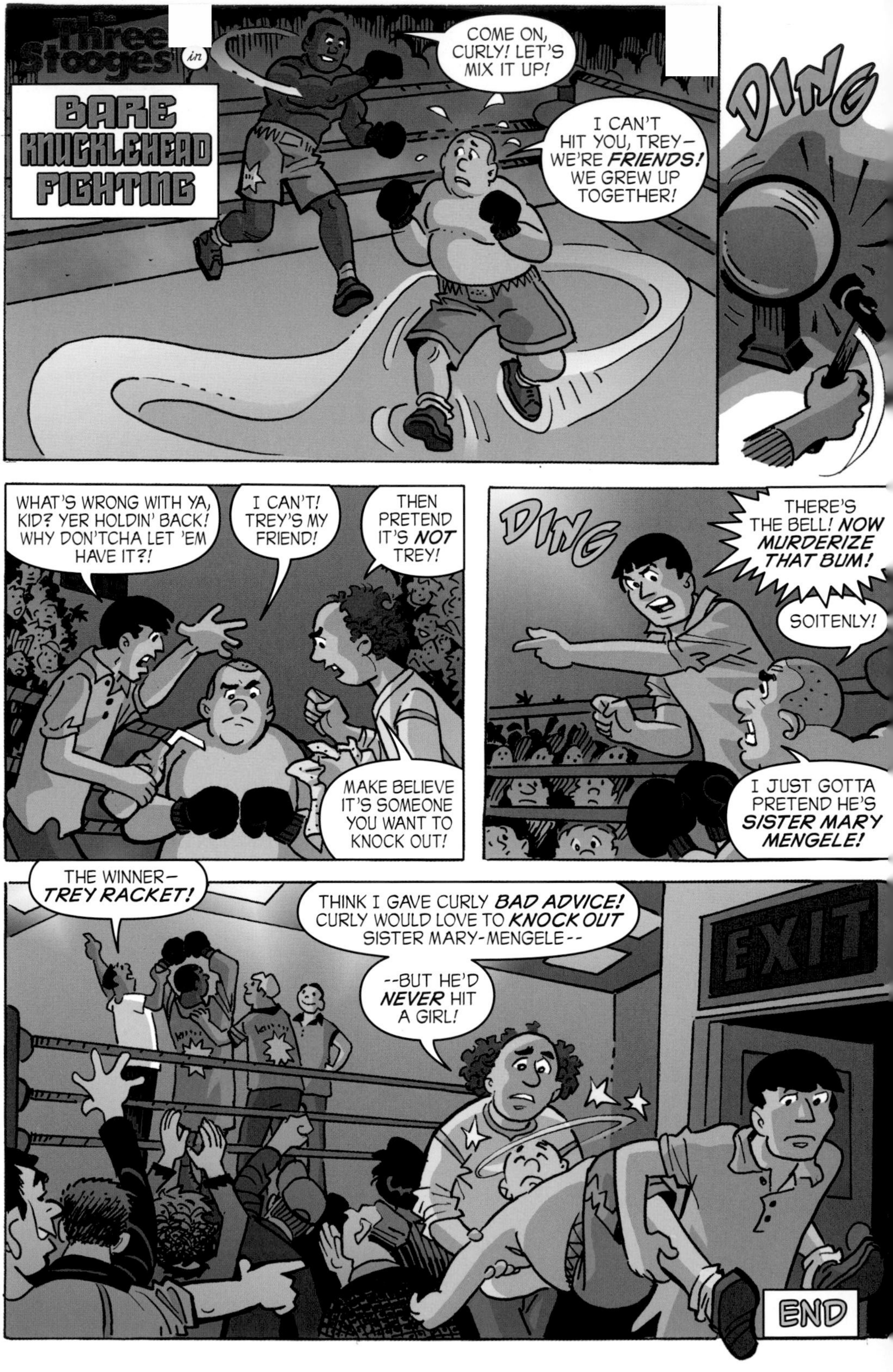
The Three Stooges in
BARE KNUCKLEHEAD FIGHTING
COME ON, CURLY! LET'S MIX IT UP!
I CAN'T HIT YOU, TREY— WE'RE FRIENDS! WE GREW UP TOGETHER!
DING
WHAT'S WRONG WITH YA, KID? YER HOLDIN' BACK! WHY DON'TCHA LET 'EM HAVE IT?!
I CAN'T! TREY'S MY FRIEND!
THEN PRETEND IT'S NOT TREY!
MAKE BELIEVE IT'S SOMEONE YOU WANT TO KNOCK OUT!
DING
THERE'S THE BELL! NOW MURDERIZE THAT BUM!
SOITENLY!
I JUST GOTTA PRETEND HE'S SISTER MARY MENGELE!
THE WINNER— TREY RACKET!
THINK I GAVE CURLY BAD ADVICE! CURLY WOULD LOVE TO KNOCK OUT SISTER MARY-MENGELE--
--BUT HE'D NEVER HIT A GIRL!
EXIT
END

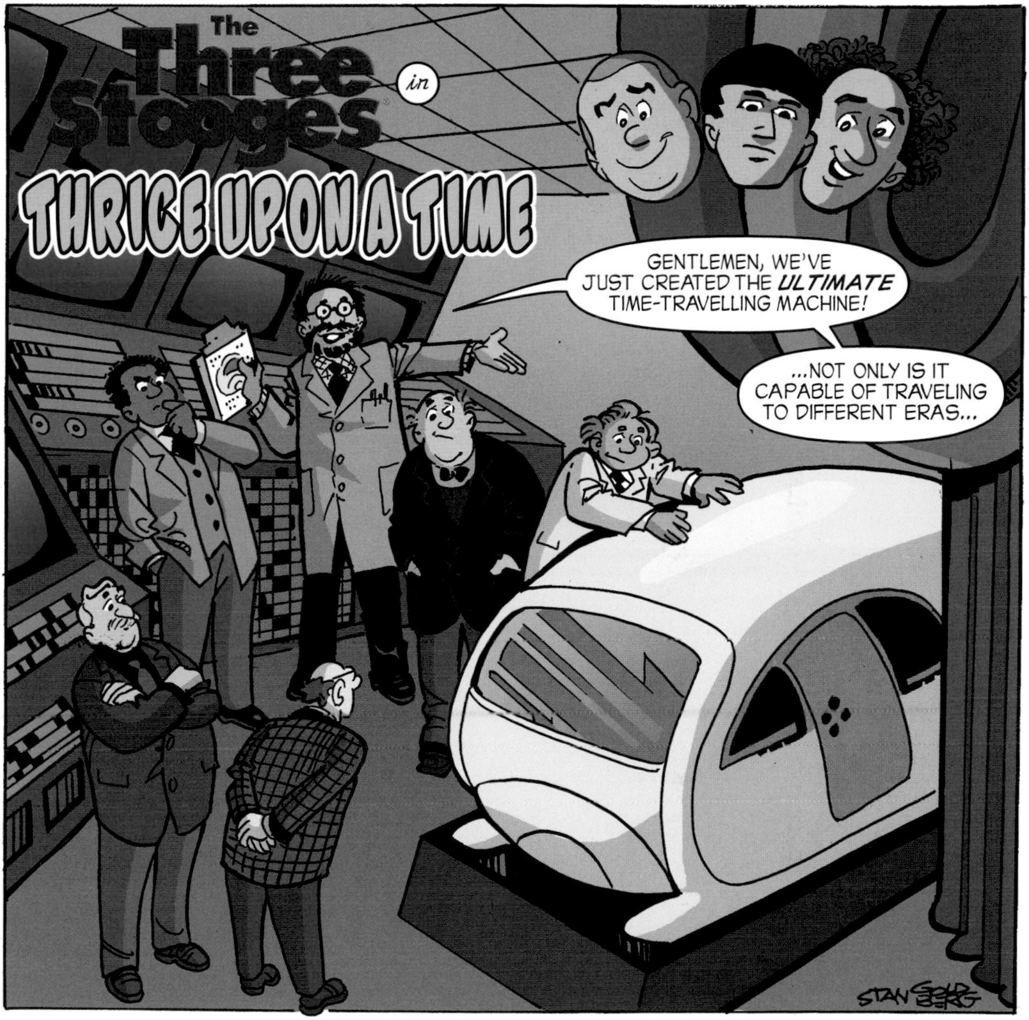
The Three Stooges in
THRICE UPON A TIME
GENTLEMEN, WE'VE JUST CREATED THE *ULTIMATE* TIME-TRAVELLING MACHINE!
...NOT ONLY IS IT CAPABLE OF TRAVELING TO DIFFERENT ERAS...
STAN GOLDBERG

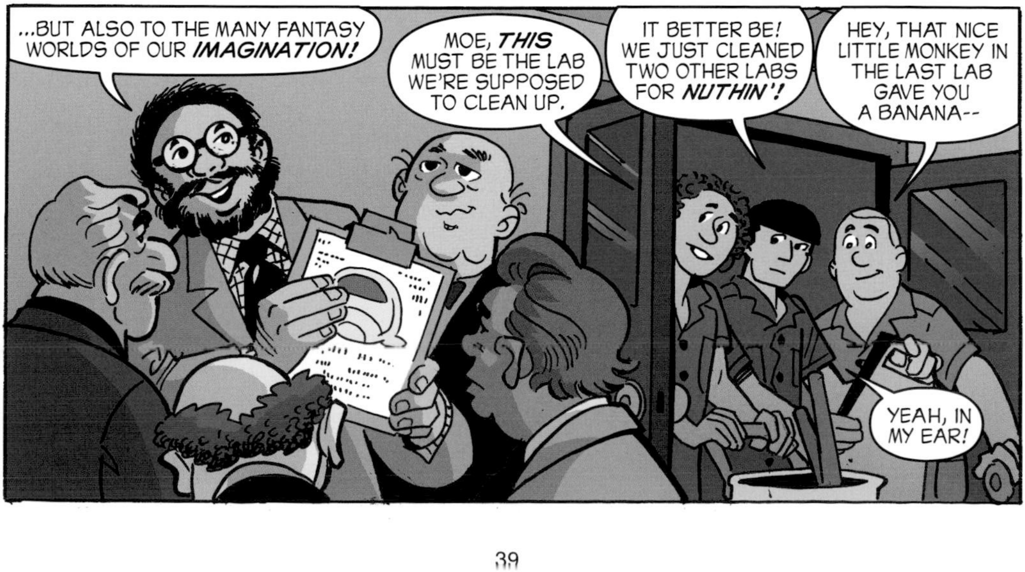
...BUT ALSO TO THE MANY FANTASY WORLDS OF OUR *IMAGINATION!*
MOE, *THIS* MUST BE THE LAB WE'RE SUPPOSED TO CLEAN UP.
IT BETTER BE! WE JUST CLEANED TWO OTHER LABS FOR *NUTHIN'!*
HEY, THAT NICE LITTLE MONKEY IN THE LAST LAB GAVE YOU A BANANA--
YEAH, IN MY EAR!

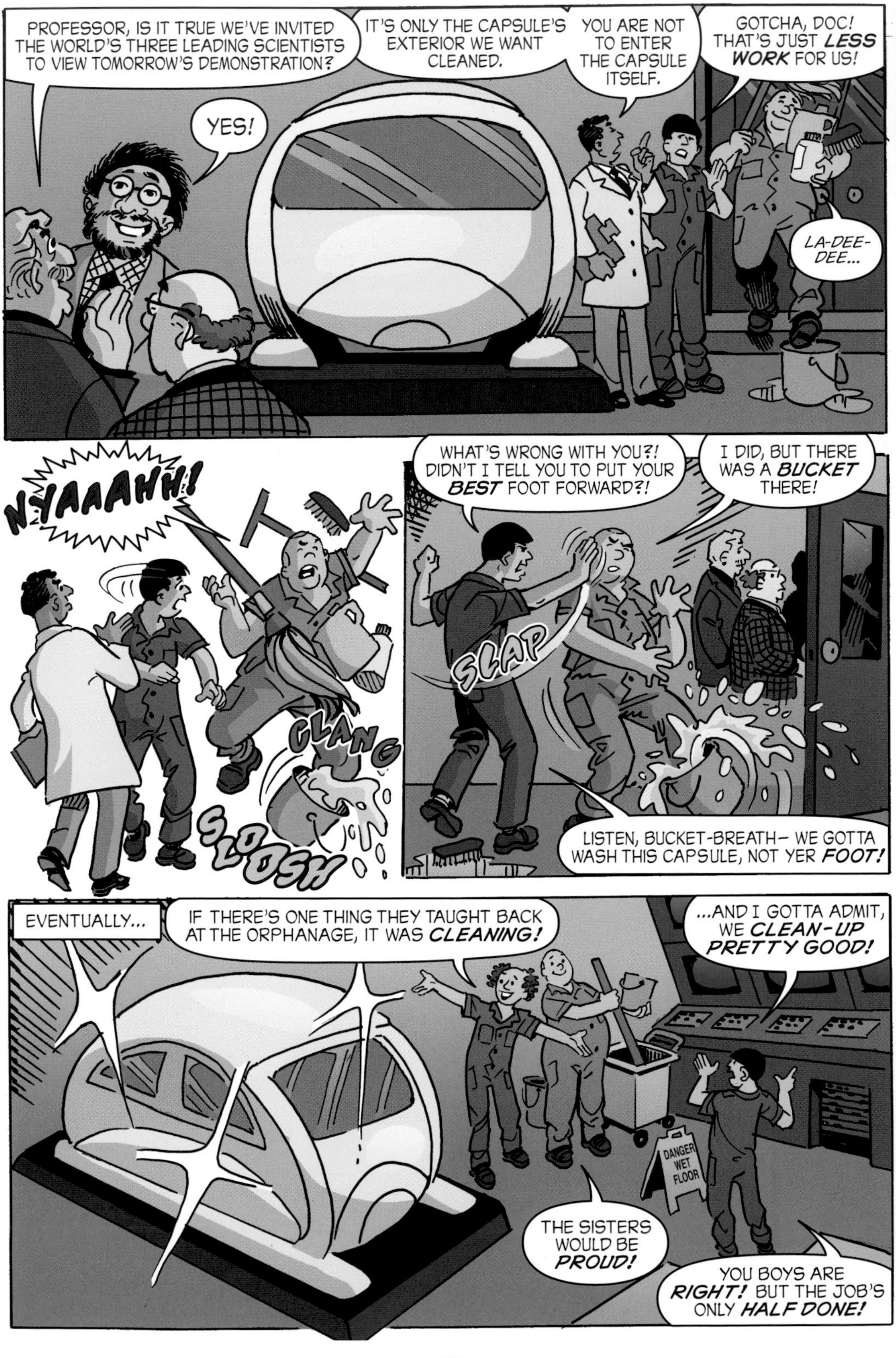
PROFESSOR, IS IT TRUE WE'VE INVITED THE WORLD'S THREE LEADING SCIENTISTS TO VIEW TOMORROW'S DEMONSTRATION?
YES!
IT'S ONLY THE CAPSULE'S EXTERIOR WE WANT CLEANED.
YOU ARE NOT TO ENTER THE CAPSULE ITSELF.
GOTCHA, DOC! THAT'S JUST LESS WORK FOR US!
LA-DEE-DEE...
NYAAAHH!
CLANG
SLOOSH
WHAT'S WRONG WITH YOU?! DIDN'T I TELL YOU TO PUT YOUR BEST FOOT FORWARD?!
I DID, BUT THERE WAS A BUCKET THERE!
SLAP
LISTEN, BUCKET-BREATH— WE GOTTA WASH THIS CAPSULE, NOT YER FOOT!
EVENTUALLY...
IF THERE'S ONE THING THEY TAUGHT BACK AT THE ORPHANAGE, IT WAS CLEANING!
...AND I GOTTA ADMIT, WE CLEAN-UP PRETTY GOOD!
DANGER WET FLOOR
THE SISTERS WOULD BE PROUD!
YOU BOYS ARE RIGHT! BUT THE JOB'S ONLY HALF DONE!

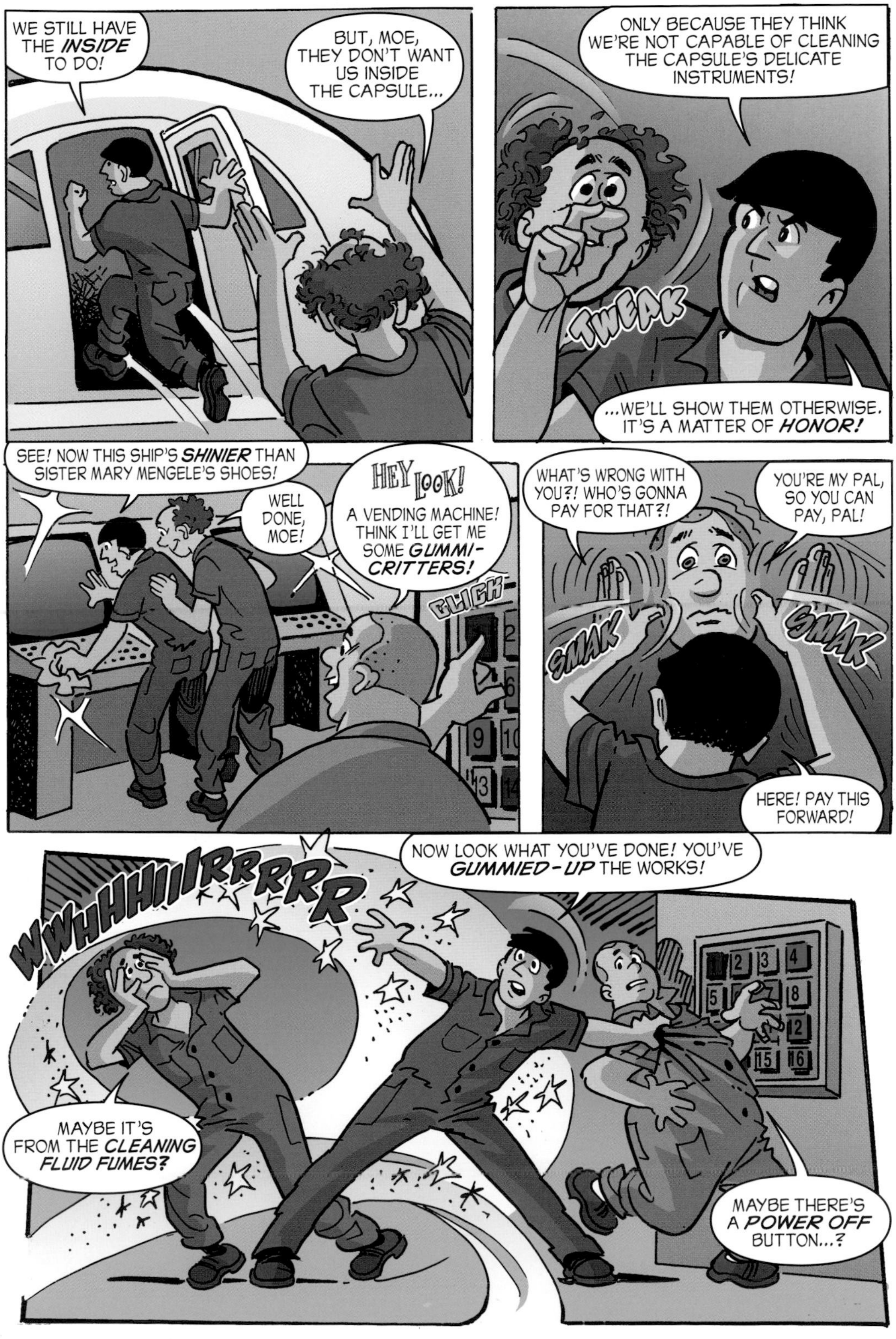
WE STILL HAVE THE INSIDE TO DO!
BUT, MOE, THEY DON'T WANT US INSIDE THE CAPSULE...
ONLY BECAUSE THEY THINK WE'RE NOT CAPABLE OF CLEANING THE CAPSULE'S DELICATE INSTRUMENTS!
TWEAK
...WE'LL SHOW THEM OTHERWISE. IT'S A MATTER OF HONOR!
SEE! NOW THIS SHIP'S SHINIER THAN SISTER MARY MENGELE'S SHOES!
WELL DONE, MOE!
HEY LOOK! A VENDING MACHINE! THINK I'LL GET ME SOME GUMMI-CRITTERS!
CLICK
WHAT'S WRONG WITH YOU?! WHO'S GONNA PAY FOR THAT?!
YOU'RE MY PAL, SO YOU CAN PAY, PAL!
SMAK
SMAK
HERE! PAY THIS FORWARD!
NOW LOOK WHAT YOU'VE DONE! YOU'VE GUMMIED-UP THE WORKS!
WWHHHIIIRRRRR
MAYBE IT'S FROM THE CLEANING FLUID FUMES?
MAYBE THERE'S A POWER OFF BUTTON...?

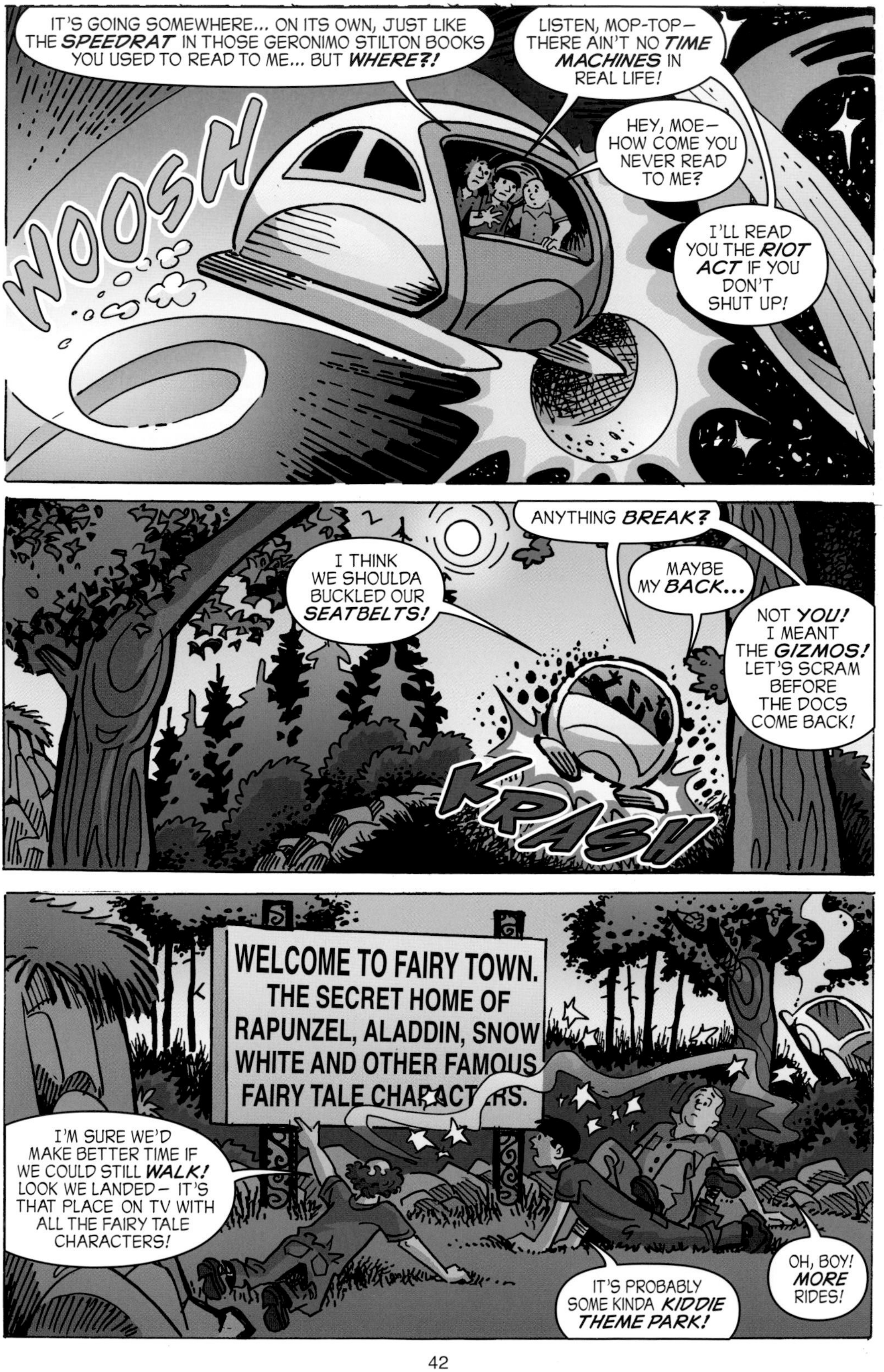
IT'S GOING SOMEWHERE... ON ITS OWN, JUST LIKE THE SPEEDRAT IN THOSE GERONIMO STILTON BOOKS YOU USED TO READ TO ME... BUT WHERE?!
LISTEN, MOP-TOP— THERE AIN'T NO TIME MACHINES IN REAL LIFE!
HEY, MOE— HOW COME YOU NEVER READ TO ME?
I'LL READ YOU THE RIOT ACT IF YOU DON'T SHUT UP!
WOOSH
ANYTHING BREAK?
I THINK WE SHOULDA BUCKLED OUR SEATBELTS!
MAYBE MY BACK...
NOT YOU! I MEANT THE GIZMOS! LET'S SCRAM BEFORE THE DOCS COME BACK!
KRASH
WELCOME TO FAIRY TOWN. THE SECRET HOME OF RAPUNZEL, ALADDIN, SNOW WHITE AND OTHER FAMOUS FAIRY TALE CHARACTERS.
I'M SURE WE'D MAKE BETTER TIME IF WE COULD STILL WALK! LOOK WE LANDED— IT'S THAT PLACE ON TV WITH ALL THE FAIRY TALE CHARACTERS!
IT'S PROBABLY SOME KINDA KIDDIE THEME PARK!
OH, BOY! MORE RIDES!

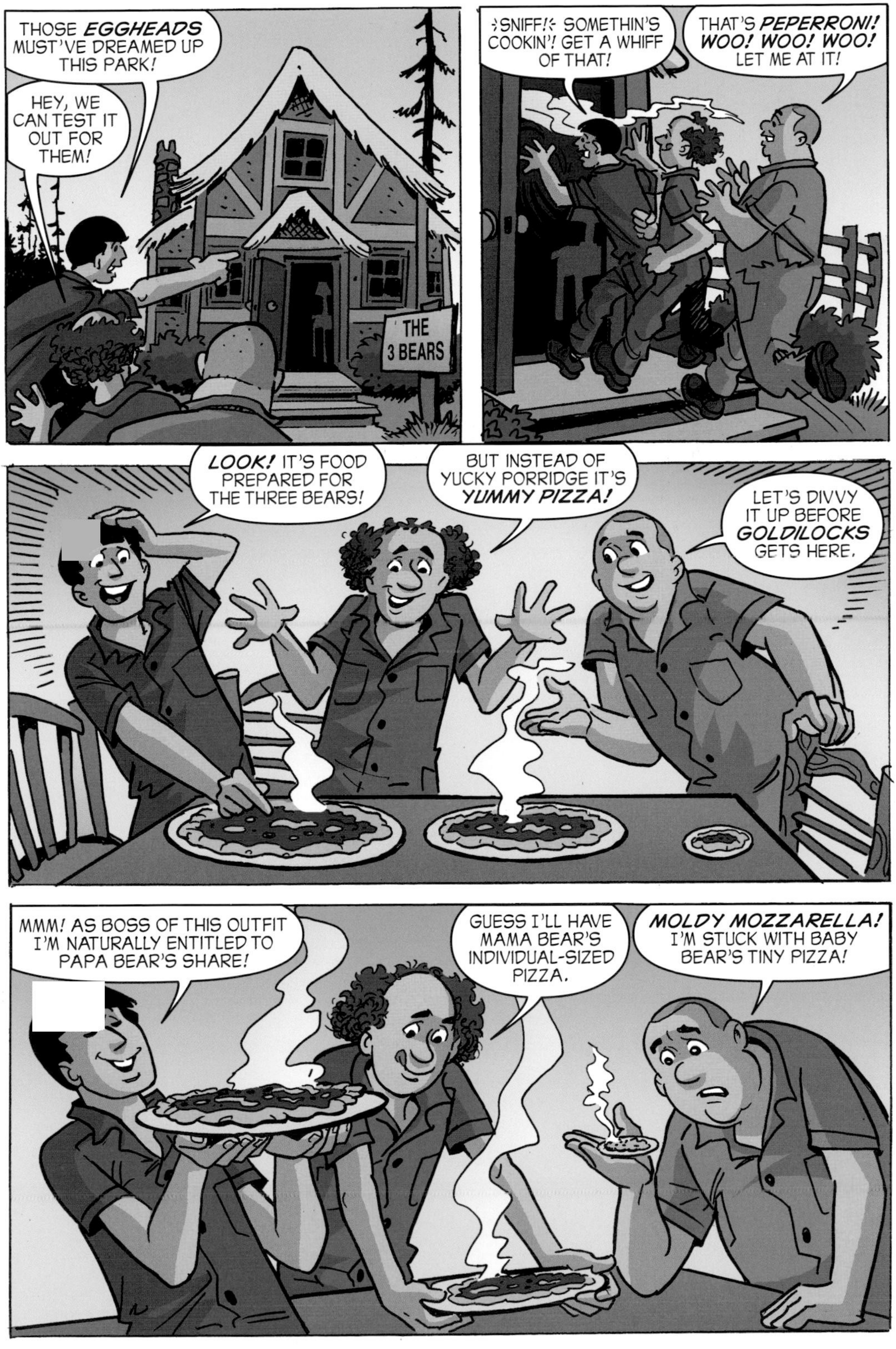
THOSE EGGHEADS MUST'VE DREAMED UP THIS PARK!
HEY, WE CAN TEST IT OUT FOR THEM!
THE 3 BEARS
SNIFF! SOMETHIN'S COOKIN'! GET A WHIFF OF THAT!
THAT'S PEPERRONI! WOO! WOO! WOO! LET ME AT IT!
LOOK! IT'S FOOD PREPARED FOR THE THREE BEARS!
BUT INSTEAD OF YUCKY PORRIDGE IT'S YUMMY PIZZA!
LET'S DIVVY IT UP BEFORE GOLDILOCKS GETS HERE.
MMM! AS BOSS OF THIS OUTFIT I'M NATURALLY ENTITLED TO PAPA BEAR'S SHARE!
GUESS I'LL HAVE MAMA BEAR'S INDIVIDUAL-SIZED PIZZA.
MOLDY MOZZARELLA! I'M STUCK WITH BABY BEAR'S TINY PIZZA!

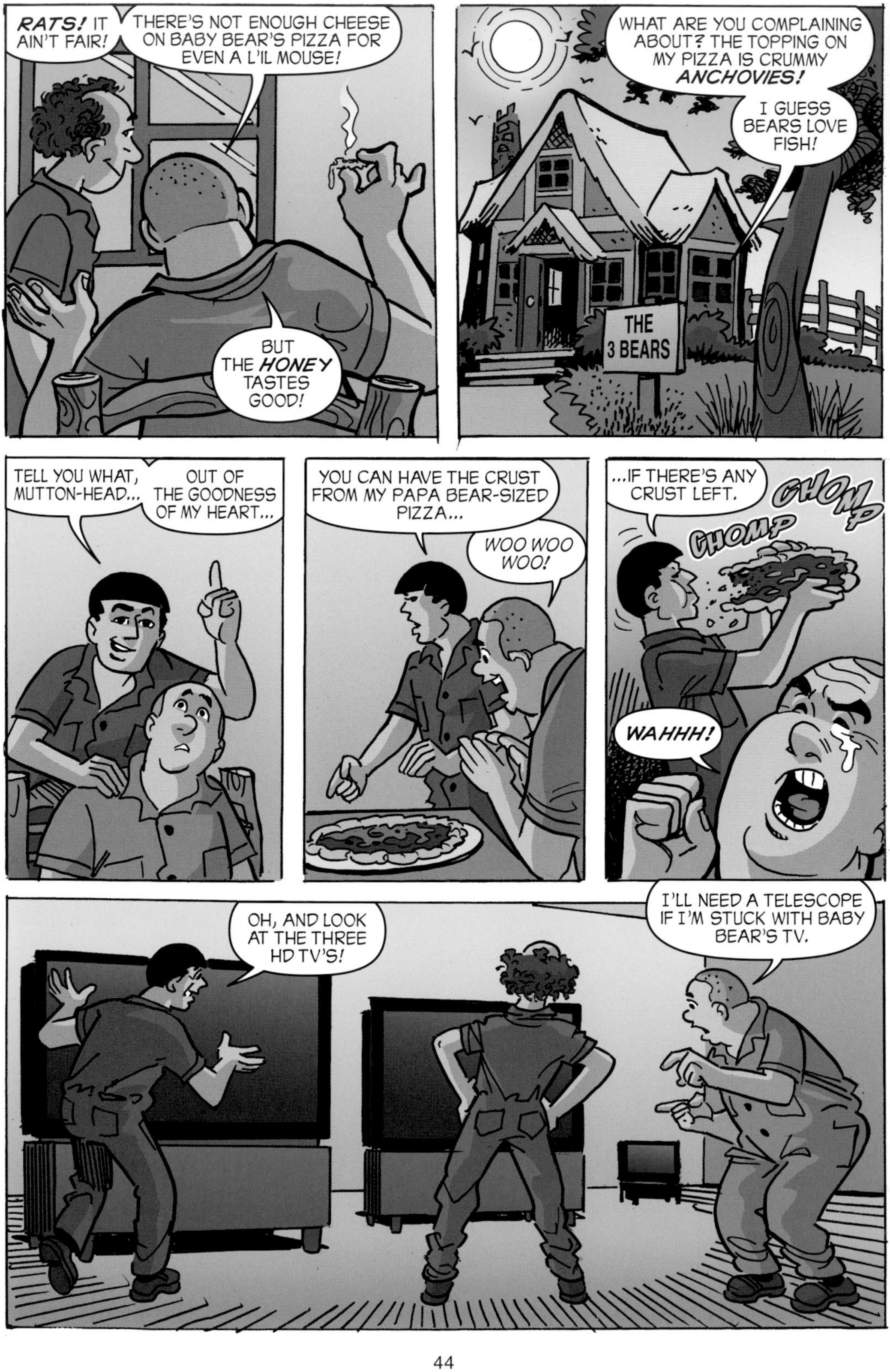
RATS! IT AIN'T FAIR!
THERE'S NOT ENOUGH CHEESE ON BABY BEAR'S PIZZA FOR EVEN A L'IL MOUSE!
BUT THE HONEY TASTES GOOD!
WHAT ARE YOU COMPLAINING ABOUT? THE TOPPING ON MY PIZZA IS CRUMMY ANCHOVIES!
I GUESS BEARS LOVE FISH!
THE 3 BEARS
TELL YOU WHAT, MUTTON-HEAD...
OUT OF THE GOODNESS OF MY HEART...
YOU CAN HAVE THE CRUST FROM MY PAPA BEAR-SIZED PIZZA...
WOO WOO WOO!
...IF THERE'S ANY CRUST LEFT.
CHOMP
CHOMP
WAHHH!
OH, AND LOOK AT THE THREE HD TV'S!
I'LL NEED A TELESCOPE IF I'M STUCK WITH BABY BEAR'S TV.

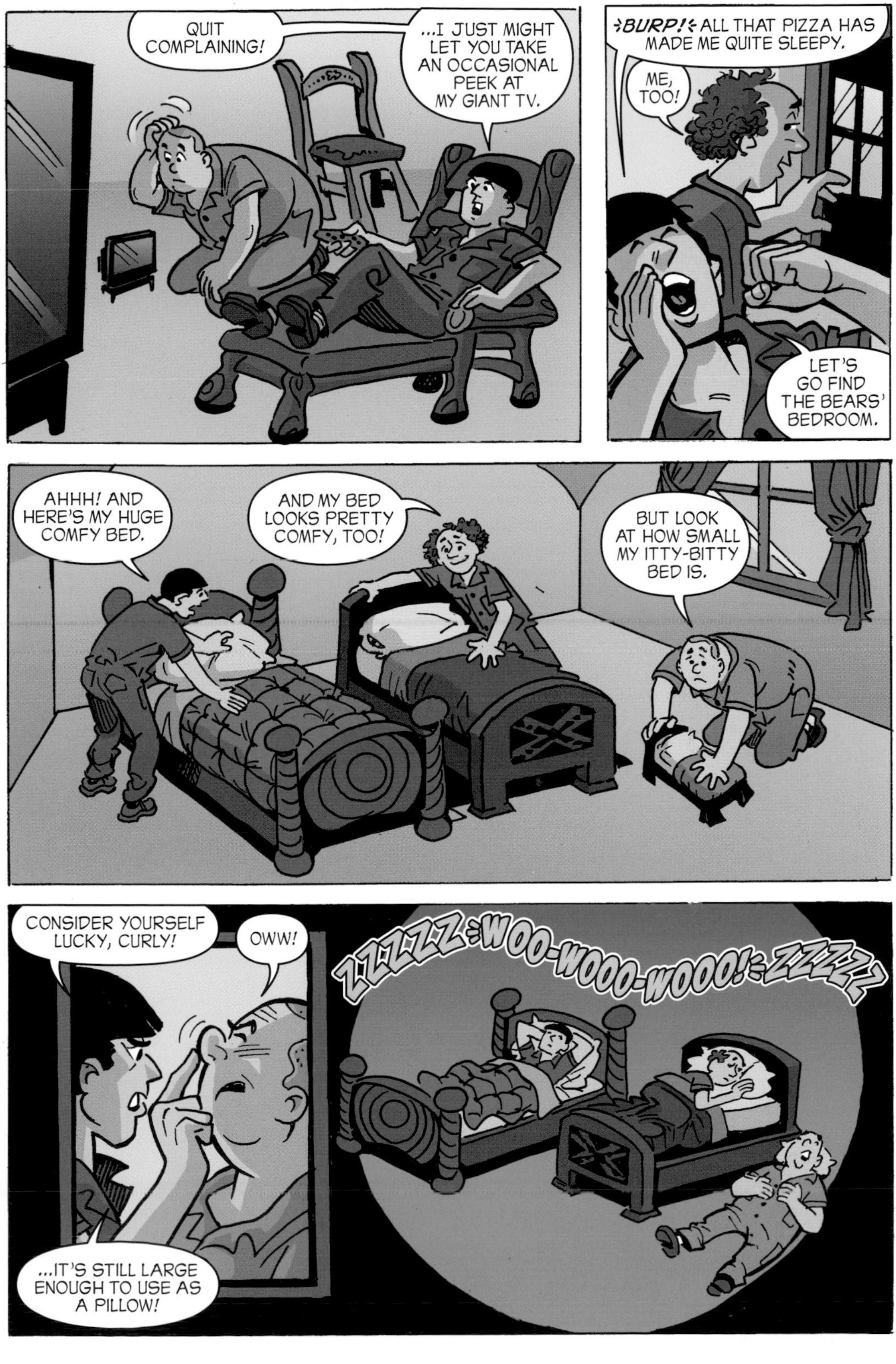
QUIT COMPLAINING!
...I JUST MIGHT LET YOU TAKE AN OCCASIONAL PEEK AT MY GIANT TV.
BURP! ALL THAT PIZZA HAS MADE ME QUITE SLEEPY.
ME, TOO!
LET'S GO FIND THE BEARS' BEDROOM.
AHHH! AND HERE'S MY HUGE COMFY BED.
AND MY BED LOOKS PRETTY COMFY, TOO!
BUT LOOK AT HOW SMALL MY ITTY-BITTY BED IS.
CONSIDER YOURSELF LUCKY, CURLY!
OWW!
...IT'S STILL LARGE ENOUGH TO USE AS A PILLOW!
ZZZZZ WOO-WOOO-WOOO! ZZZZZ

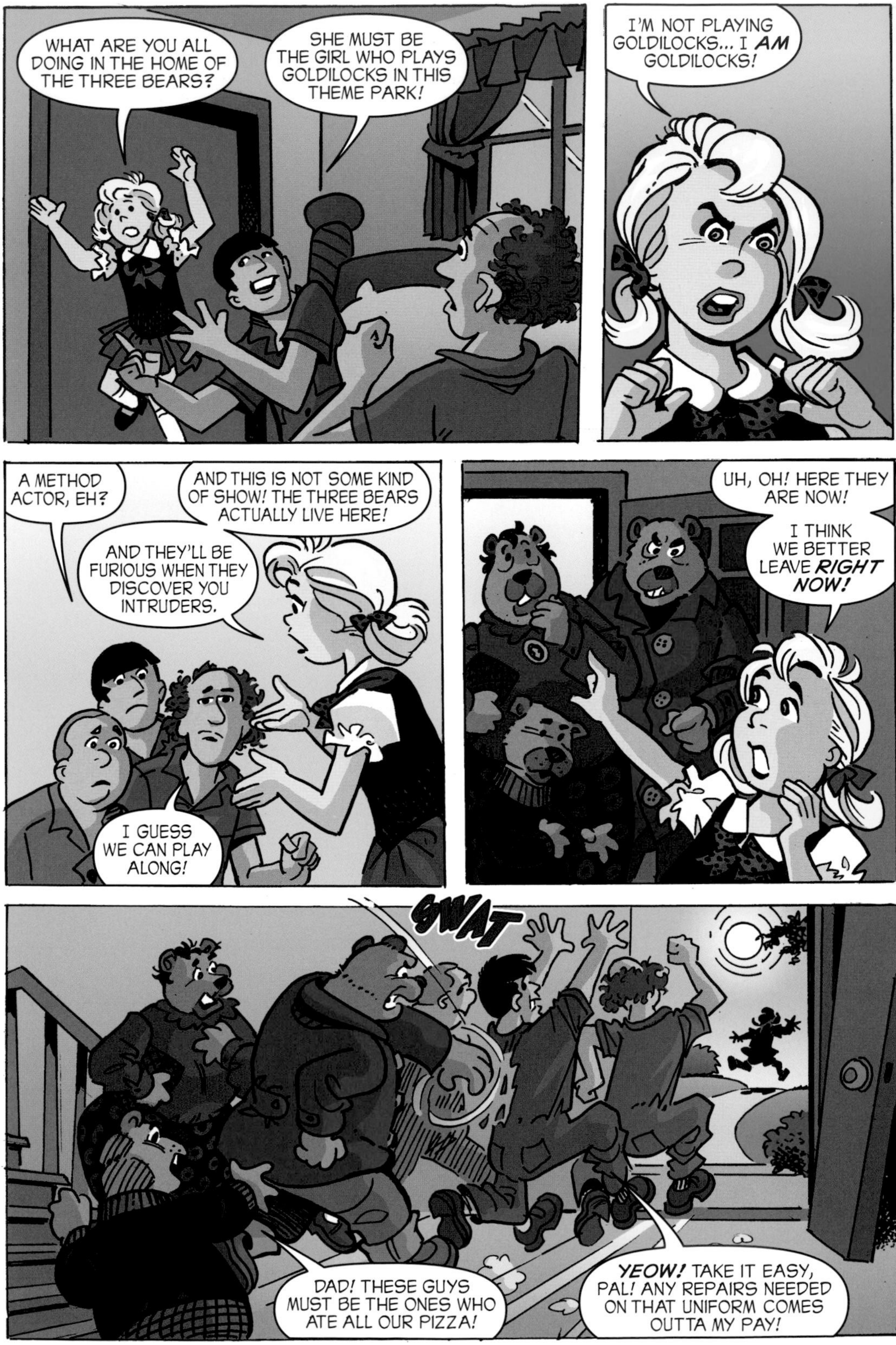
WHAT ARE YOU ALL DOING IN THE HOME OF THE THREE BEARS?
SHE MUST BE THE GIRL WHO PLAYS GOLDILOCKS IN THIS THEME PARK!
I'M NOT PLAYING GOLDILOCKS... I AM GOLDILOCKS!
A METHOD ACTOR, EH?
AND THIS IS NOT SOME KIND OF SHOW! THE THREE BEARS ACTUALLY LIVE HERE!
AND THEY'LL BE FURIOUS WHEN THEY DISCOVER YOU INTRUDERS.
I GUESS WE CAN PLAY ALONG!
UH, OH! HERE THEY ARE NOW!
I THINK WE BETTER LEAVE RIGHT NOW!
SWAT
DAD! THESE GUYS MUST BE THE ONES WHO ATE ALL OUR PIZZA!
YEOW! TAKE IT EASY, PAL! ANY REPAIRS NEEDED ON THAT UNIFORM COMES OUTTA MY PAY!

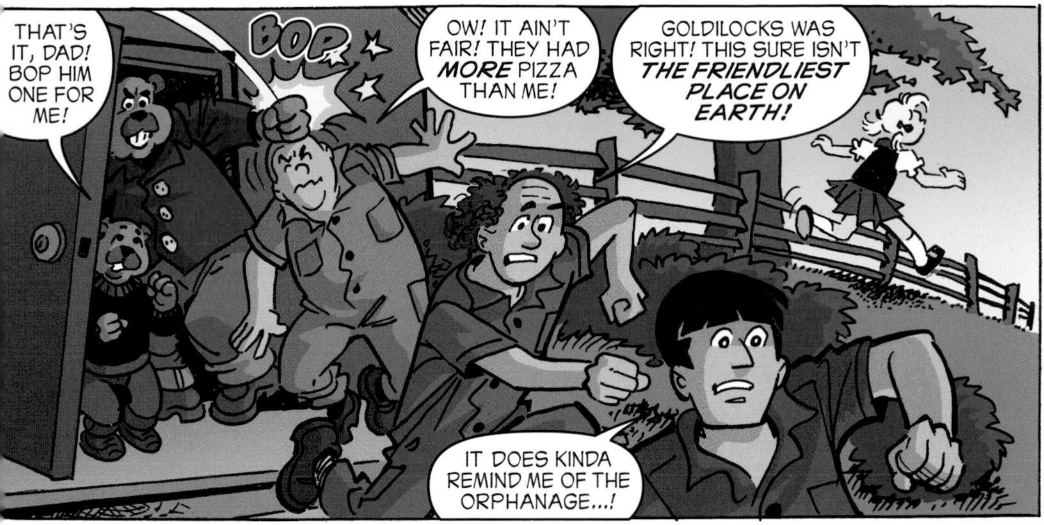
THAT'S IT, DAD! BOP HIM ONE FOR ME!
BOP
OW! IT AIN'T FAIR! THEY HAD MORE PIZZA THAN ME!
GOLDILOCKS WAS RIGHT! THIS SURE ISN'T THE FRIENDLIEST PLACE ON EARTH!
IT DOES KINDA REMIND ME OF THE ORPHANAGE...!

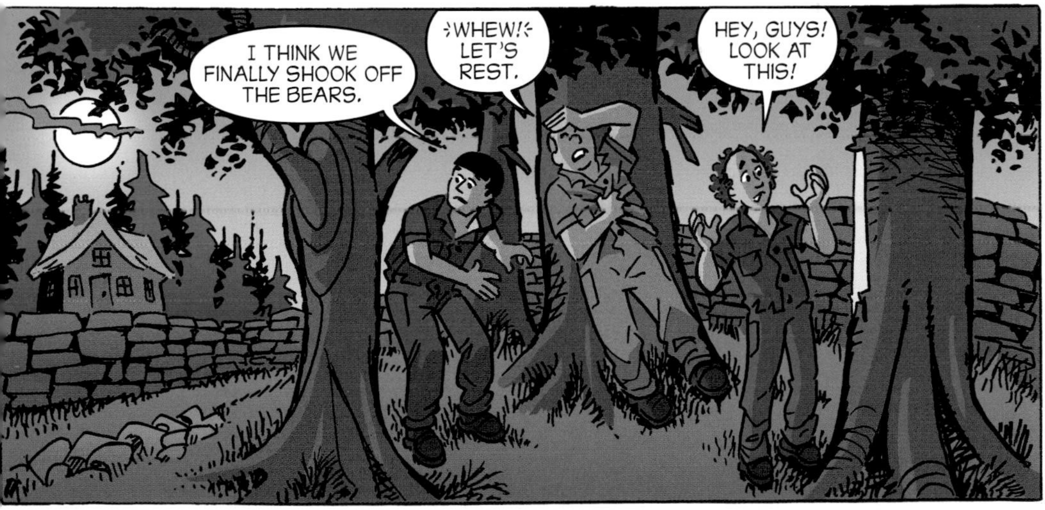
I THINK WE FINALLY SHOOK OFF THE BEARS.
WHEW! LET'S REST.
HEY, GUYS! LOOK AT THIS!

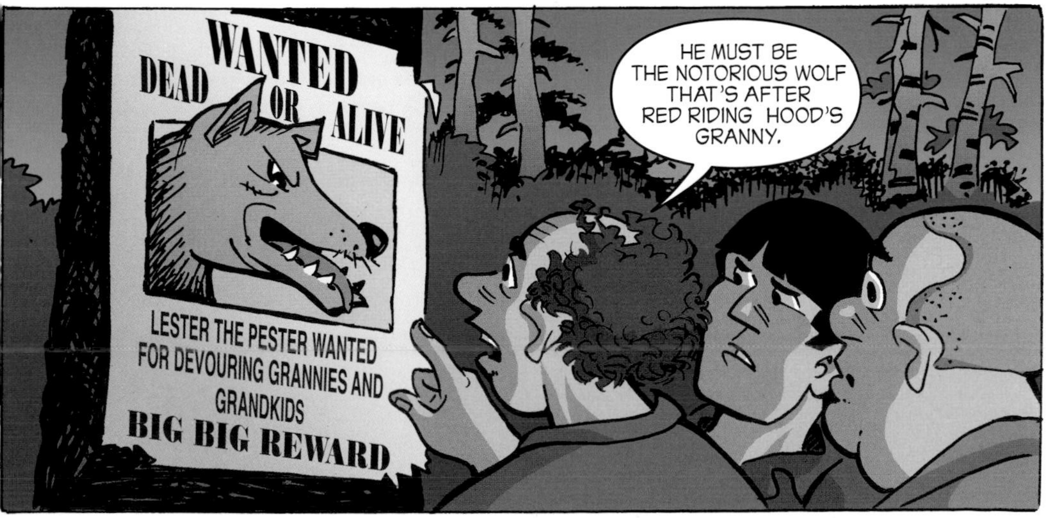
WANTED
DEAD OR ALIVE
LESTER THE PESTER WANTED FOR DEVOURING GRANNIES AND GRANDKIDS
BIG BIG REWARD
HE MUST BE THE NOTORIOUS WOLF THAT'S AFTER RED RIDING HOOD'S GRANNY.

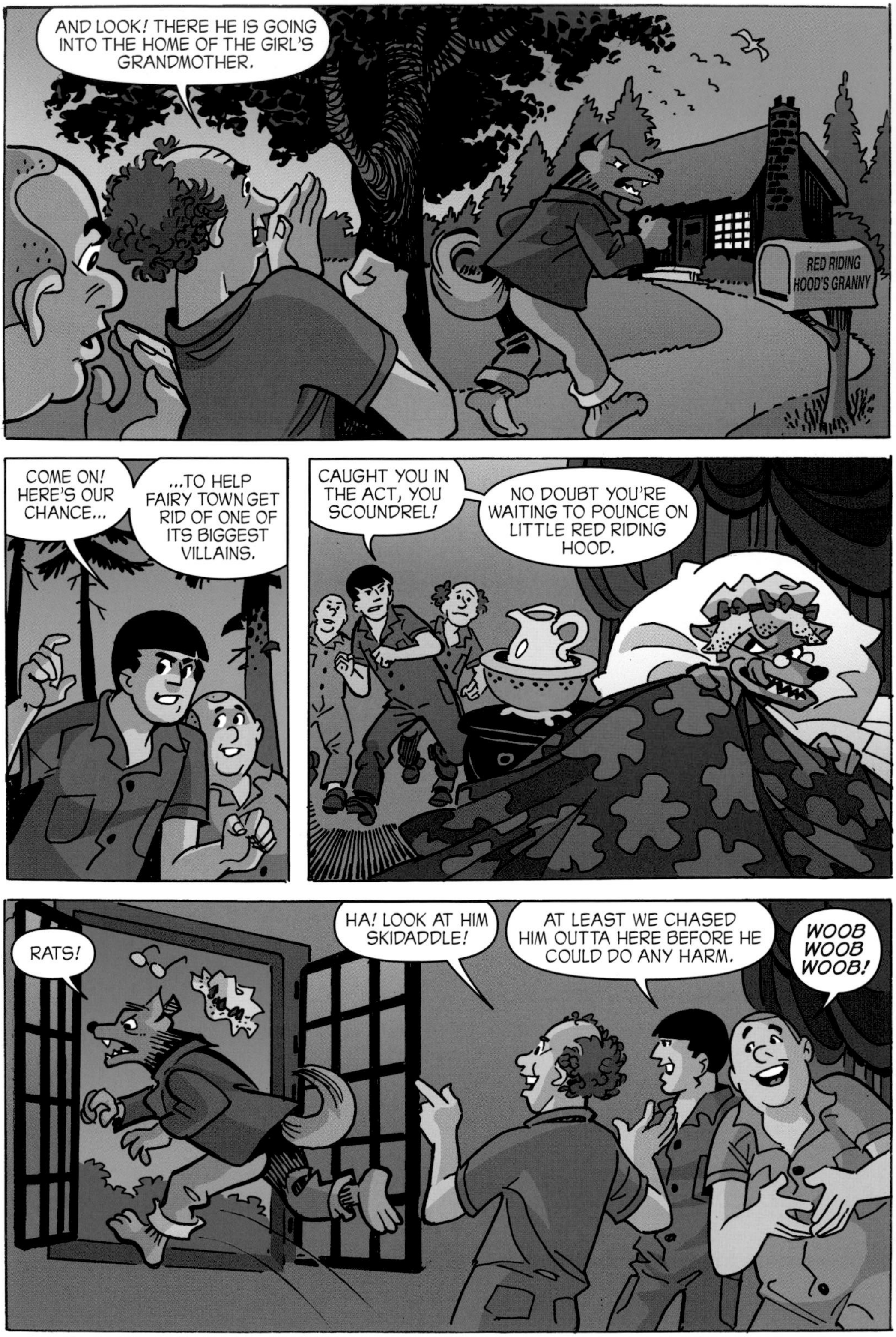
AND LOOK! THERE HE IS GOING INTO THE HOME OF THE GIRL'S GRANDMOTHER.
RED RIDING HOOD'S GRANNY
COME ON! HERE'S OUR CHANCE...
...TO HELP FAIRY TOWN GET RID OF ONE OF ITS BIGGEST VILLAINS.
CAUGHT YOU IN THE ACT, YOU SCOUNDREL!
NO DOUBT YOU'RE WAITING TO POUNCE ON LITTLE RED RIDING HOOD.
RATS!
HA! LOOK AT HIM SKIDADDLE!
AT LEAST WE CHASED HIM OUTTA HERE BEFORE HE COULD DO ANY HARM.
WOOB WOOB WOOB!

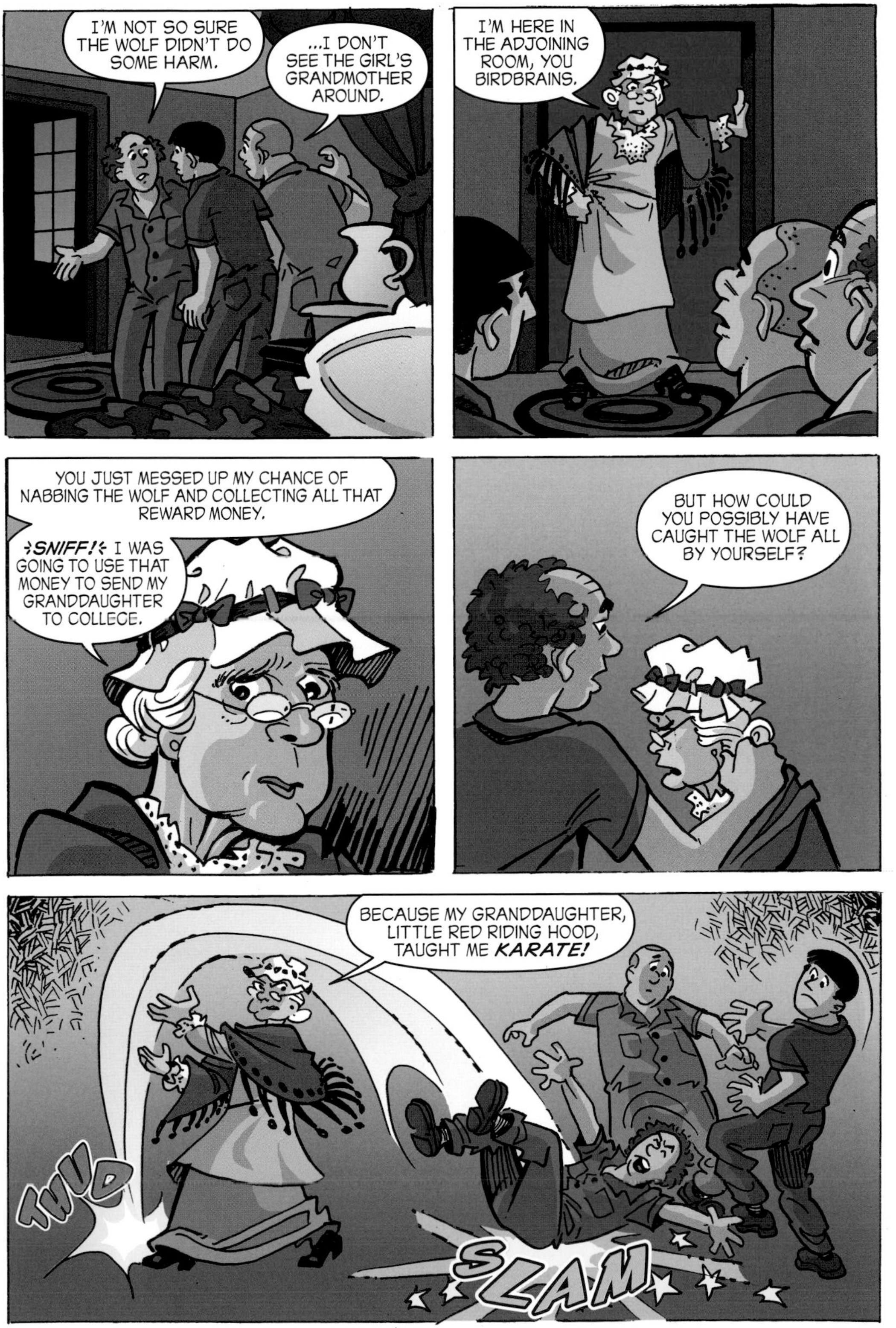
I'M NOT SO SURE THE WOLF DIDN'T DO SOME HARM.
...I DON'T SEE THE GIRL'S GRANDMOTHER AROUND.
I'M HERE IN THE ADJOINING ROOM, YOU BIRDBRAINS.
YOU JUST MESSED UP MY CHANCE OF NABBING THE WOLF AND COLLECTING ALL THAT REWARD MONEY.
SNIFF! I WAS GOING TO USE THAT MONEY TO SEND MY GRANDDAUGHTER TO COLLEGE.
BUT HOW COULD YOU POSSIBLY HAVE CAUGHT THE WOLF ALL BY YOURSELF?
BECAUSE MY GRANDDAUGHTER, LITTLE RED RIDING HOOD, TAUGHT ME *KARATE!*
THUD
SLAM

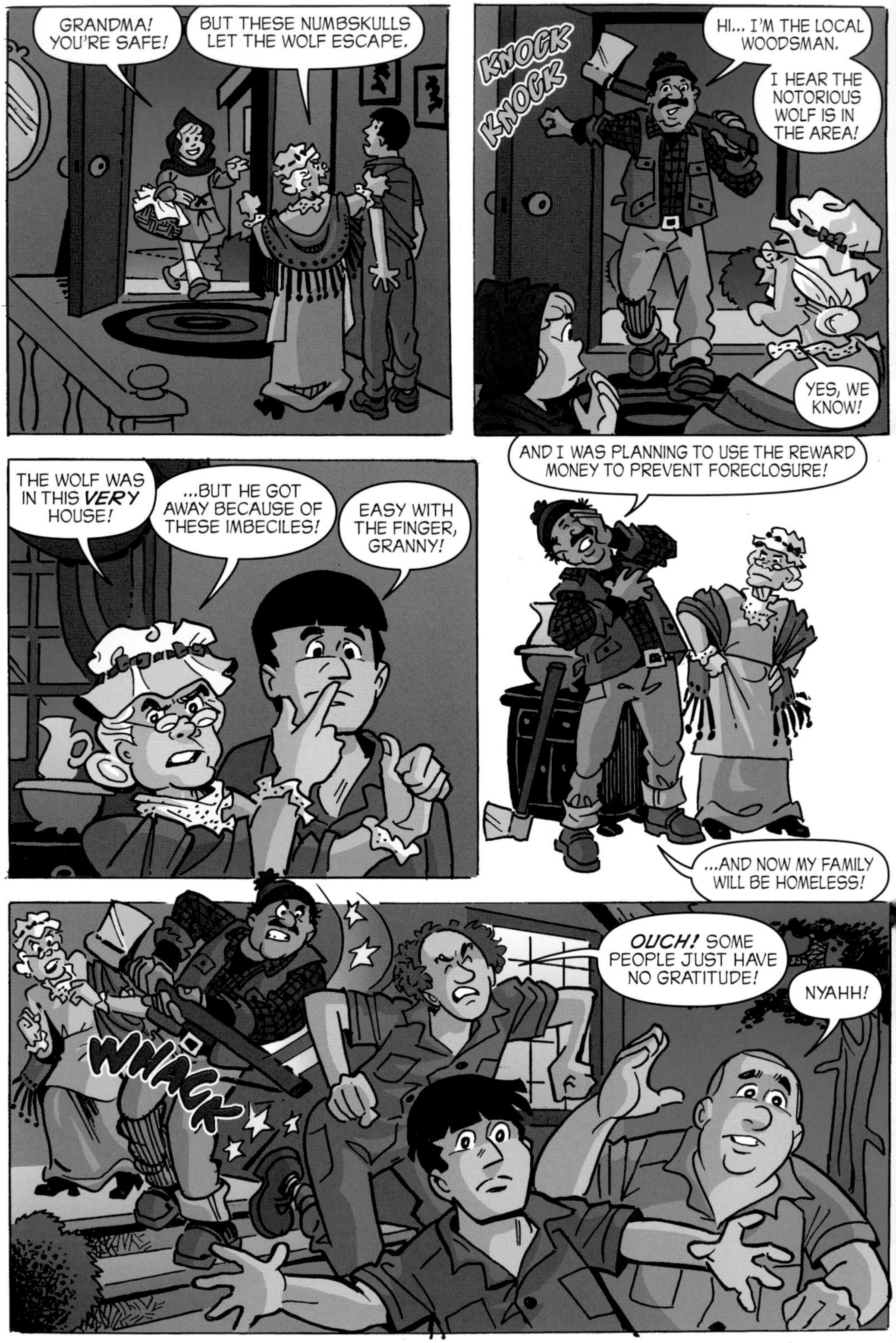
GRANDMA! YOU'RE SAFE!
BUT THESE NUMBSKULLS LET THE WOLF ESCAPE.
KNOCK KNOCK
HI... I'M THE LOCAL WOODSMAN.
I HEAR THE NOTORIOUS WOLF IS IN THE AREA!
YES, WE KNOW!
THE WOLF WAS IN THIS VERY HOUSE!
...BUT HE GOT AWAY BECAUSE OF THESE IMBECILES!
EASY WITH THE FINGER, GRANNY!
AND I WAS PLANNING TO USE THE REWARD MONEY TO PREVENT FORECLOSURE!
...AND NOW MY FAMILY WILL BE HOMELESS!
WHACK
OUCH! SOME PEOPLE JUST HAVE NO GRATITUDE!
NYAHH!

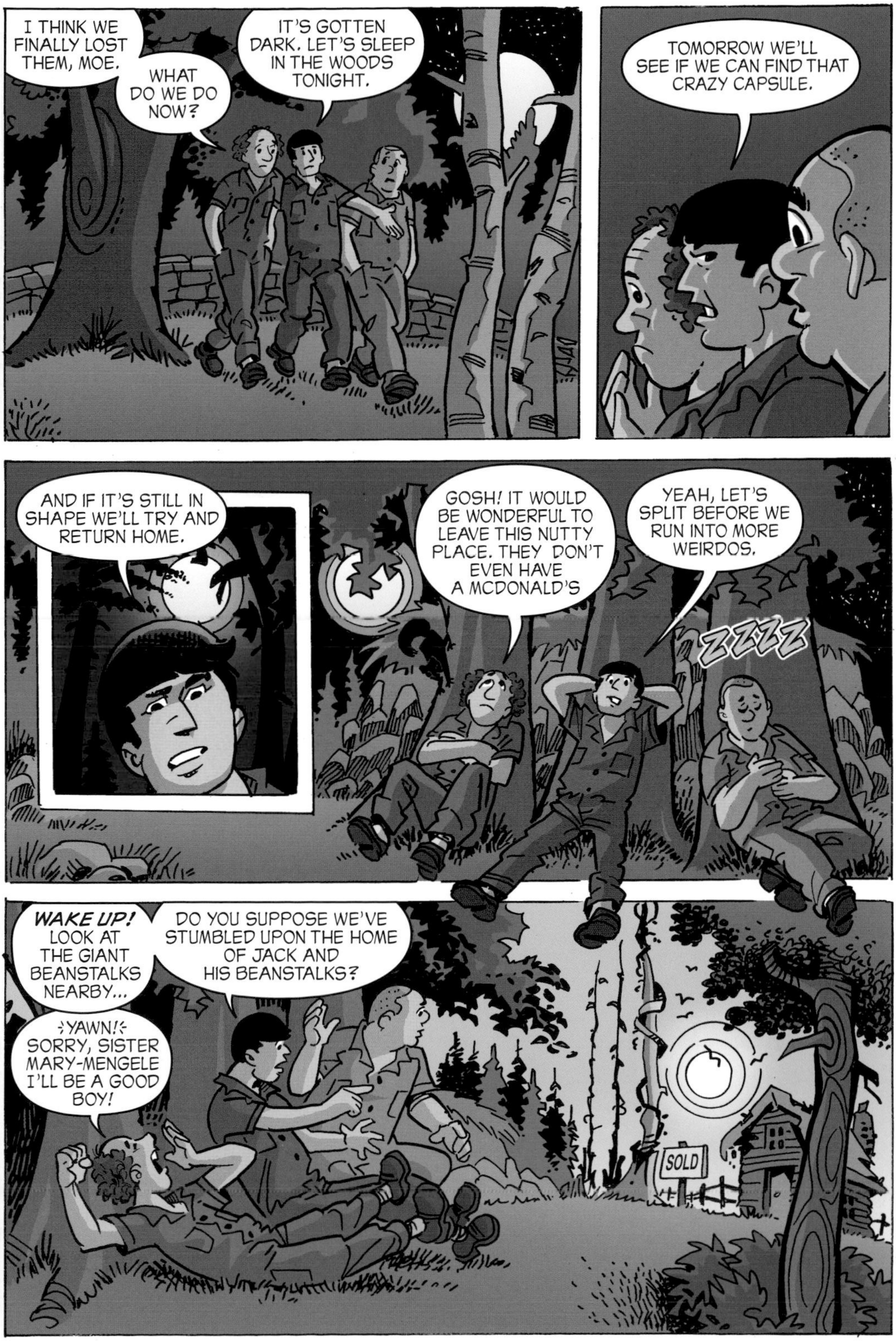
I THINK WE FINALLY LOST THEM, MOE.
WHAT DO WE DO NOW?
IT'S GOTTEN DARK. LET'S SLEEP IN THE WOODS TONIGHT.
TOMORROW WE'LL SEE IF WE CAN FIND THAT CRAZY CAPSULE.
AND IF IT'S STILL IN SHAPE WE'LL TRY AND RETURN HOME.
GOSH! IT WOULD BE WONDERFUL TO LEAVE THIS NUTTY PLACE. THEY DON'T EVEN HAVE A MCDONALD'S
YEAH, LET'S SPLIT BEFORE WE RUN INTO MORE WEIRDOS.
ZZZZ
WAKE UP! LOOK AT THE GIANT BEANSTALKS NEARBY...
DO YOU SUPPOSE WE'VE STUMBLED UPON THE HOME OF JACK AND HIS BEANSTALKS?
YAWN! SORRY, SISTER MARY-MENGELE I'LL BE A GOOD BOY!
SOLD

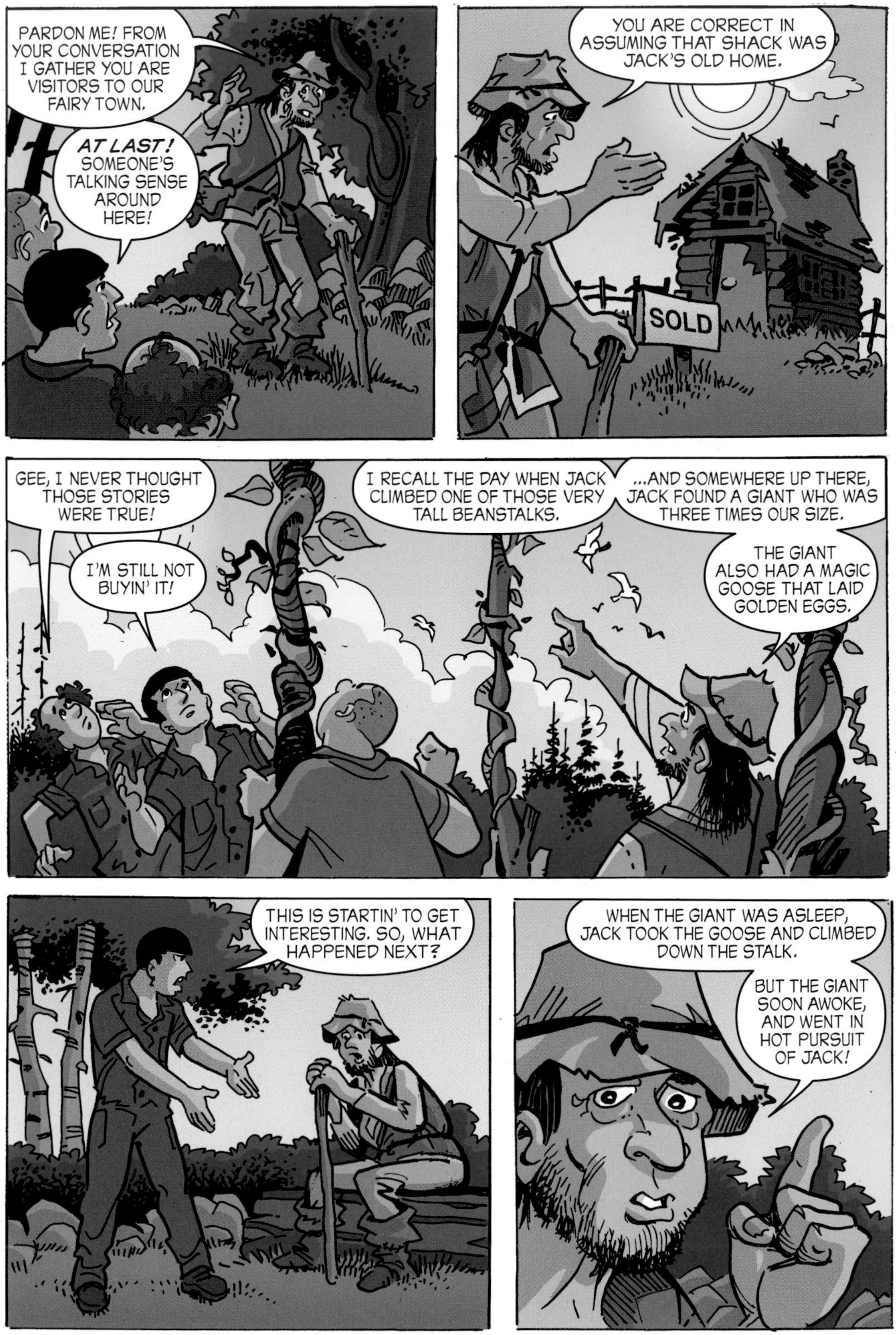
PARDON ME! FROM YOUR CONVERSATION I GATHER YOU ARE VISITORS TO OUR FAIRY TOWN.
AT LAST! SOMEONE'S TALKING SENSE AROUND HERE!
YOU ARE CORRECT IN ASSUMING THAT SHACK WAS JACK'S OLD HOME.
SOLD
GEE, I NEVER THOUGHT THOSE STORIES WERE TRUE!
I'M STILL NOT BUYIN' IT!
I RECALL THE DAY WHEN JACK CLIMBED ONE OF THOSE VERY TALL BEANSTALKS.
...AND SOMEWHERE UP THERE, JACK FOUND A GIANT WHO WAS THREE TIMES OUR SIZE.
THE GIANT ALSO HAD A MAGIC GOOSE THAT LAID GOLDEN EGGS.
THIS IS STARTIN' TO GET INTERESTING. SO, WHAT HAPPENED NEXT?
WHEN THE GIANT WAS ASLEEP, JACK TOOK THE GOOSE AND CLIMBED DOWN THE STALK.
BUT THE GIANT SOON AWOKE, AND WENT IN HOT PURSUIT OF JACK!

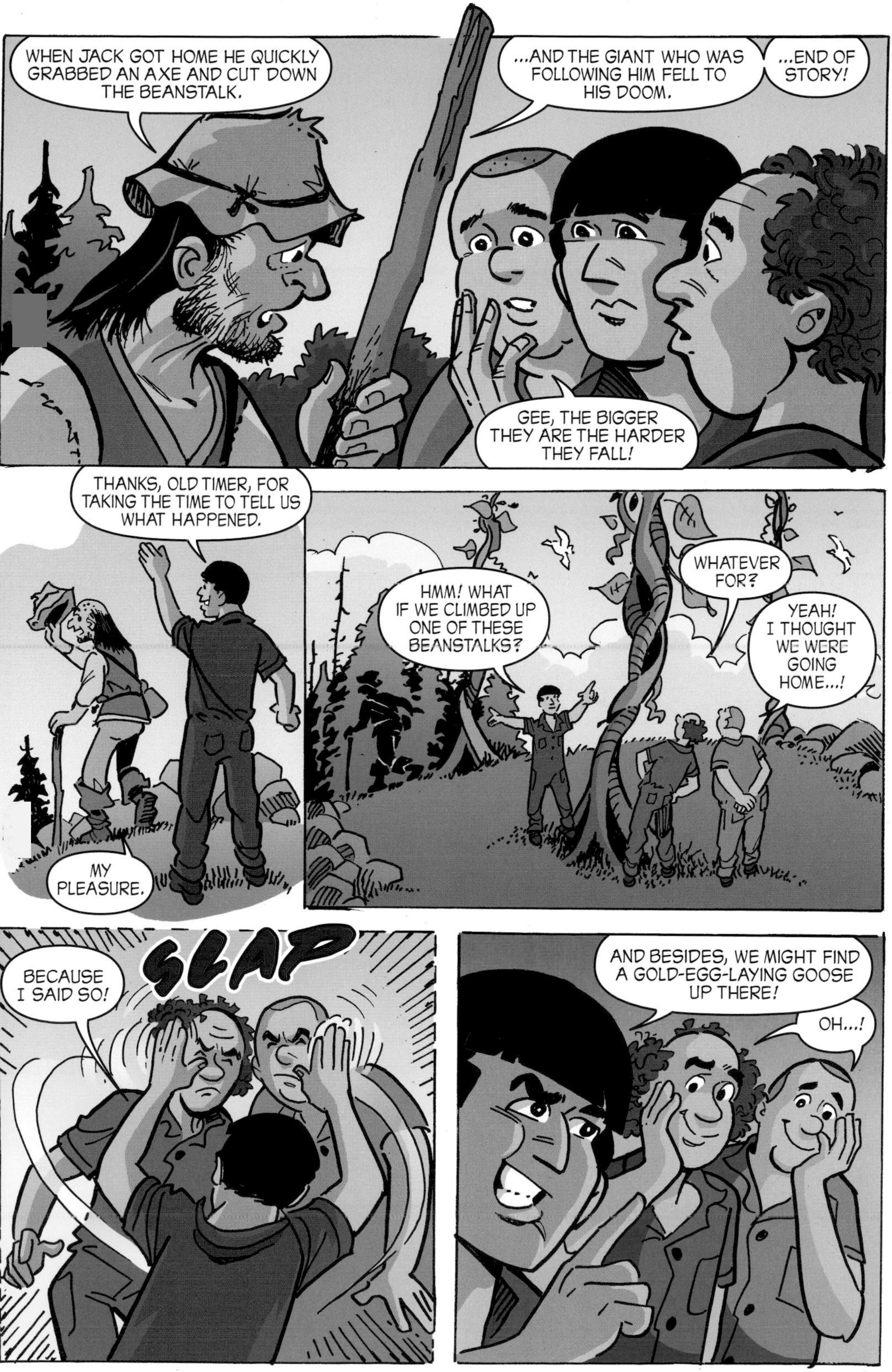
WHEN JACK GOT HOME HE QUICKLY GRABBED AN AXE AND CUT DOWN THE BEANSTALK.
...AND THE GIANT WHO WAS FOLLOWING HIM FELL TO HIS DOOM.
...END OF STORY!
GEE, THE BIGGER THEY ARE THE HARDER THEY FALL!
THANKS, OLD TIMER, FOR TAKING THE TIME TO TELL US WHAT HAPPENED.
MY PLEASURE.
HMM! WHAT IF WE CLIMBED UP ONE OF THESE BEANSTALKS?
WHATEVER FOR?
YEAH! I THOUGHT WE WERE GOING HOME...!
BECAUSE I SAID SO!
SLAP
AND BESIDES, WE MIGHT FIND A GOLD-EGG-LAYING GOOSE UP THERE!
OH...!

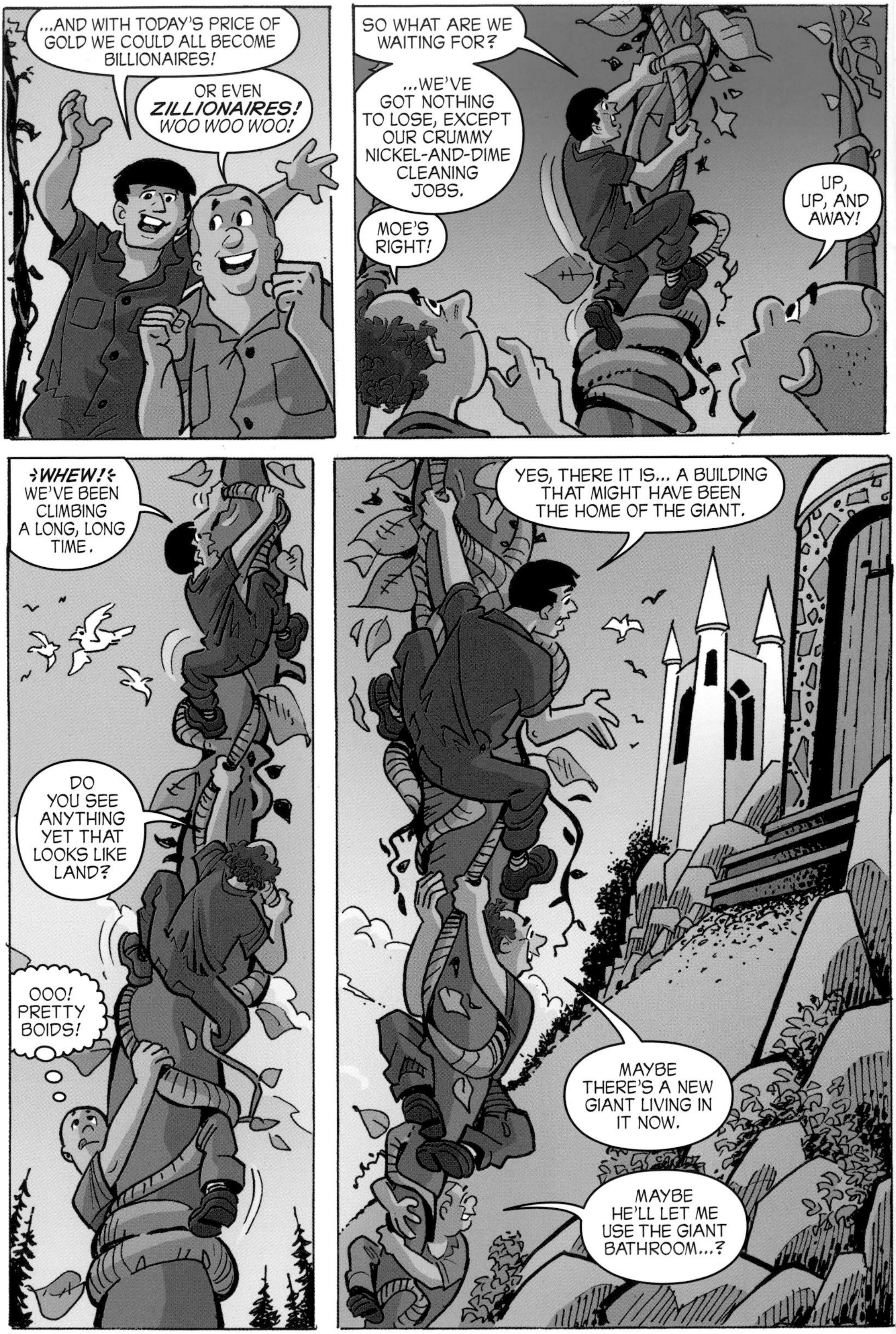
...AND WITH TODAY'S PRICE OF GOLD WE COULD ALL BECOME BILLIONAIRES!
OR EVEN ZILLIONAIRES! WOO WOO WOO!
SO WHAT ARE WE WAITING FOR?
...WE'VE GOT NOTHING TO LOSE, EXCEPT OUR CRUMMY NICKEL-AND-DIME CLEANING JOBS.
MOE'S RIGHT!
UP, UP, AND AWAY!
WHEW! WE'VE BEEN CLIMBING A LONG, LONG TIME.
DO YOU SEE ANYTHING YET THAT LOOKS LIKE LAND?
OOO! PRETTY BOIDS!
YES, THERE IT IS... A BUILDING THAT MIGHT HAVE BEEN THE HOME OF THE GIANT.
MAYBE THERE'S A NEW GIANT LIVING IN IT NOW.
MAYBE HE'LL LET ME USE THE GIANT BATHROOM...?

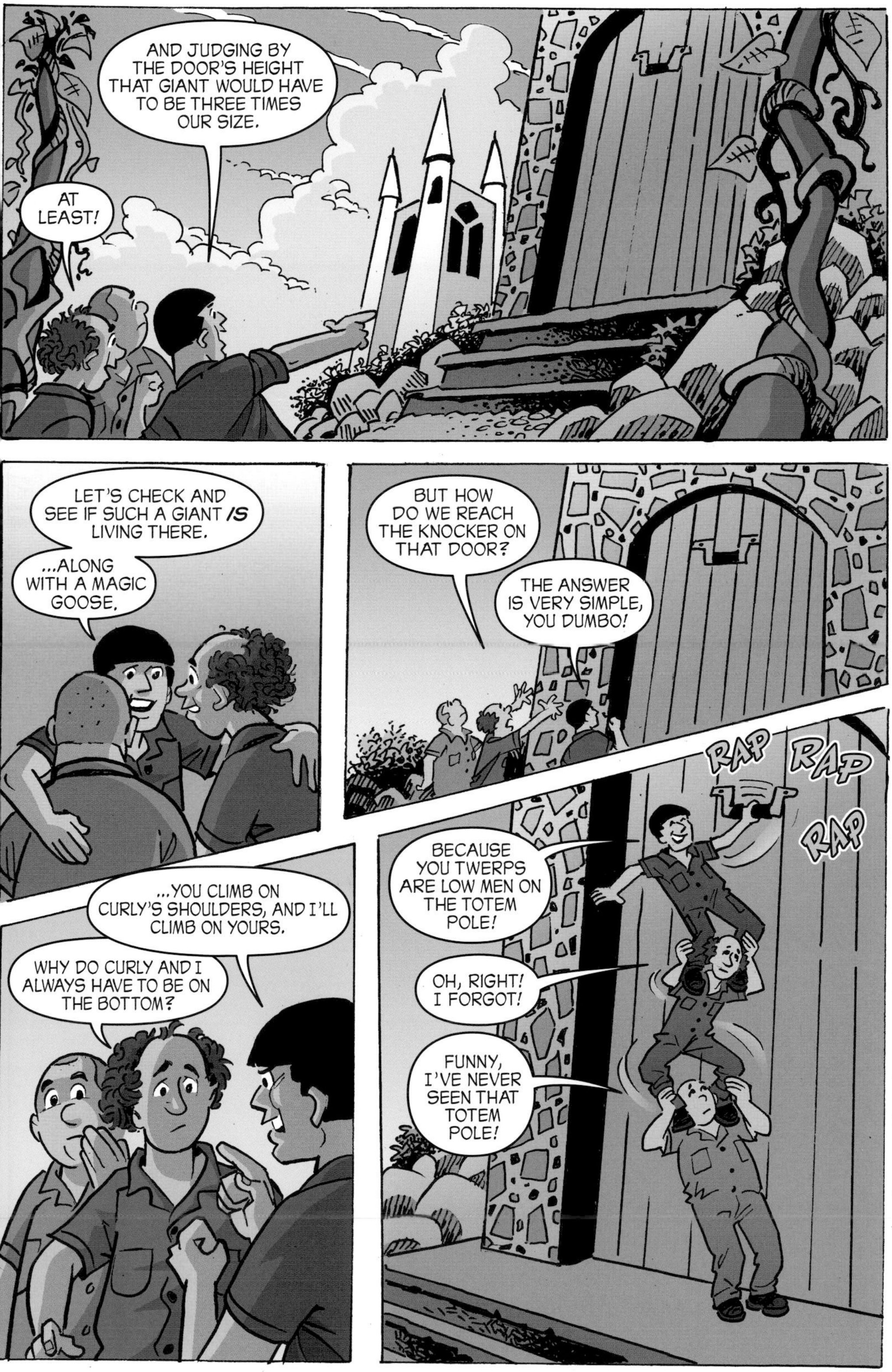
AND JUDGING BY THE DOOR'S HEIGHT THAT GIANT WOULD HAVE TO BE THREE TIMES OUR SIZE.
AT LEAST!
LET'S CHECK AND SEE IF SUCH A GIANT *IS* LIVING THERE.
...ALONG WITH A MAGIC GOOSE.
BUT HOW DO WE REACH THE KNOCKER ON THAT DOOR?
THE ANSWER IS VERY SIMPLE, YOU DUMBO!
...YOU CLIMB ON CURLY'S SHOULDERS, AND I'LL CLIMB ON YOURS.
WHY DO CURLY AND I ALWAYS HAVE TO BE ON THE BOTTOM?
RAP RAP RAP
BECAUSE YOU TWERPS ARE LOW MEN ON THE TOTEM POLE!
OH, RIGHT! I FORGOT!
FUNNY, I'VE NEVER SEEN THAT TOTEM POLE!

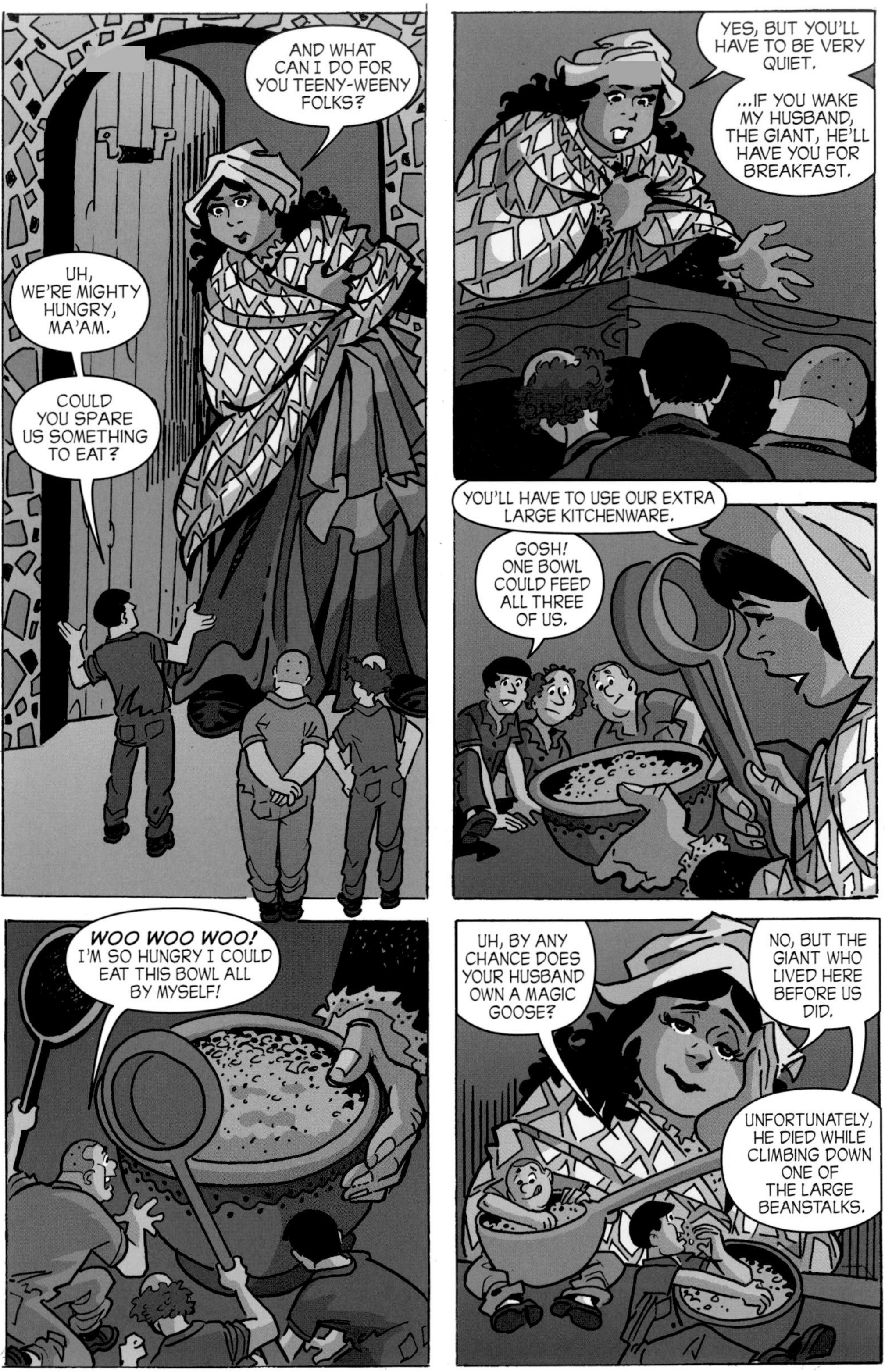
AND WHAT CAN I DO FOR YOU TEENY-WEENY FOLKS?
UH, WE'RE MIGHTY HUNGRY, MA'AM.
COULD YOU SPARE US SOMETHING TO EAT?
YES, BUT YOU'LL HAVE TO BE VERY QUIET.
...IF YOU WAKE MY HUSBAND, THE GIANT, HE'LL HAVE YOU FOR BREAKFAST.
YOU'LL HAVE TO USE OUR EXTRA LARGE KITCHENWARE.
GOSH! ONE BOWL COULD FEED ALL THREE OF US.
WOO WOO WOO! I'M SO HUNGRY I COULD EAT THIS BOWL ALL BY MYSELF!
UH, BY ANY CHANCE DOES YOUR HUSBAND OWN A MAGIC GOOSE?
NO, BUT THE GIANT WHO LIVED HERE BEFORE US DID.
UNFORTUNATELY, HE DIED WHILE CLIMBING DOWN ONE OF THE LARGE BEANSTALKS.

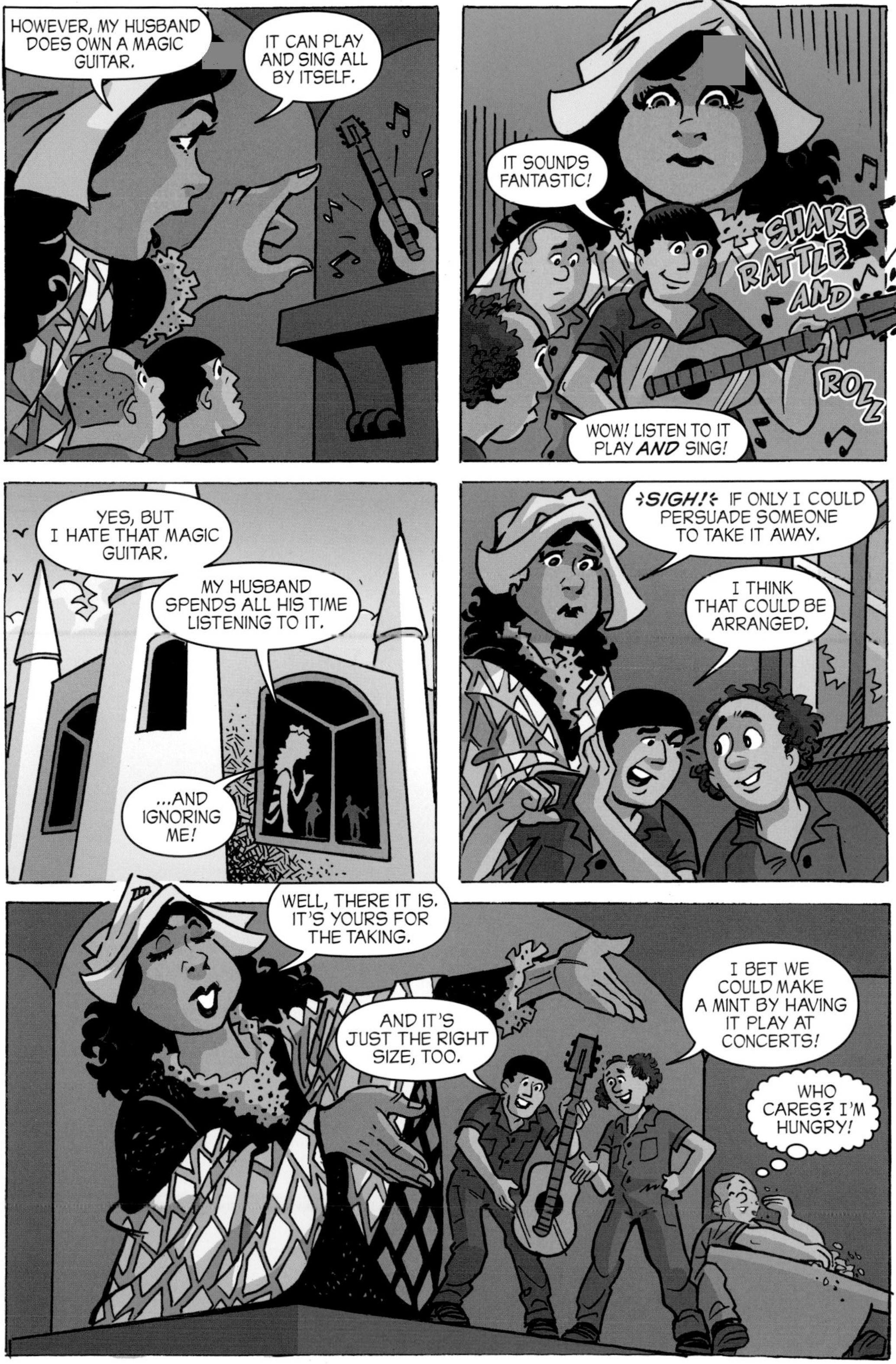

HOWEVER, MY HUSBAND DOES OWN A MAGIC GUITAR.
IT CAN PLAY AND SING ALL BY ITSELF.
IT SOUNDS FANTASTIC!
SHAKE RATTLE AND ROLL
WOW! LISTEN TO IT PLAY *AND* SING!
YES, BUT I HATE THAT MAGIC GUITAR.
MY HUSBAND SPENDS ALL HIS TIME LISTENING TO IT.
...AND IGNORING ME!
SIGH! IF ONLY I COULD PERSUADE SOMEONE TO TAKE IT AWAY.
I THINK THAT COULD BE ARRANGED.
WELL, THERE IT IS. IT'S YOURS FOR THE TAKING.
AND IT'S JUST THE RIGHT SIZE, TOO.
I BET WE COULD MAKE A MINT BY HAVING IT PLAY AT CONCERTS!
WHO CARES? I'M HUNGRY!

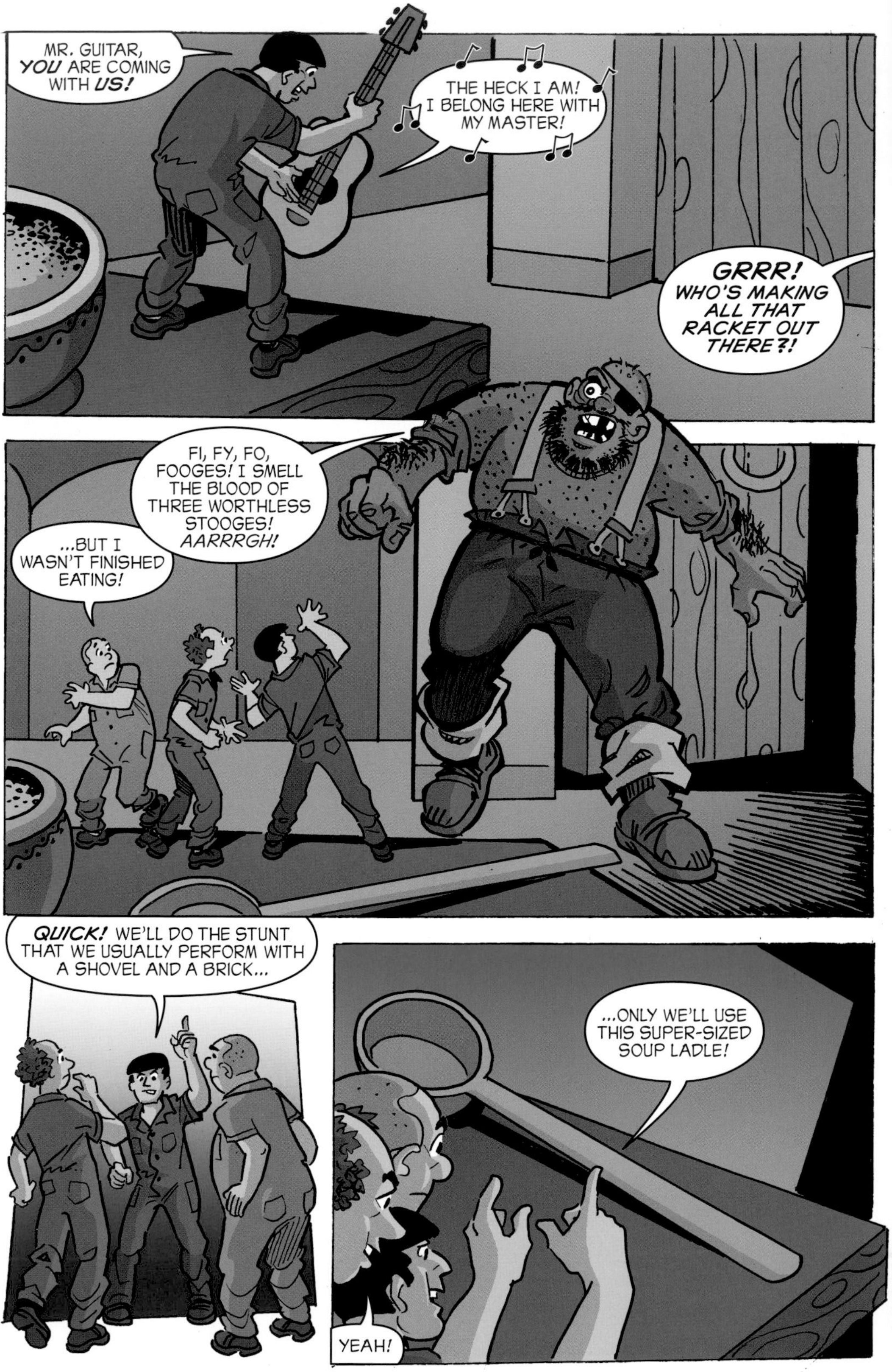
MR. GUITAR, YOU ARE COMING WITH US!
THE HECK I AM! I BELONG HERE WITH MY MASTER!
GRRR! WHO'S MAKING ALL THAT RACKET OUT THERE?!
FI, FY, FO, FOOGES! I SMELL THE BLOOD OF THREE WORTHLESS STOOGES! AARRRGH!
...BUT I WASN'T FINISHED EATING!
QUICK! WE'LL DO THE STUNT THAT WE USUALLY PERFORM WITH A SHOVEL AND A BRICK...
...ONLY WE'LL USE THIS SUPER-SIZED SOUP LADLE!
YEAH!

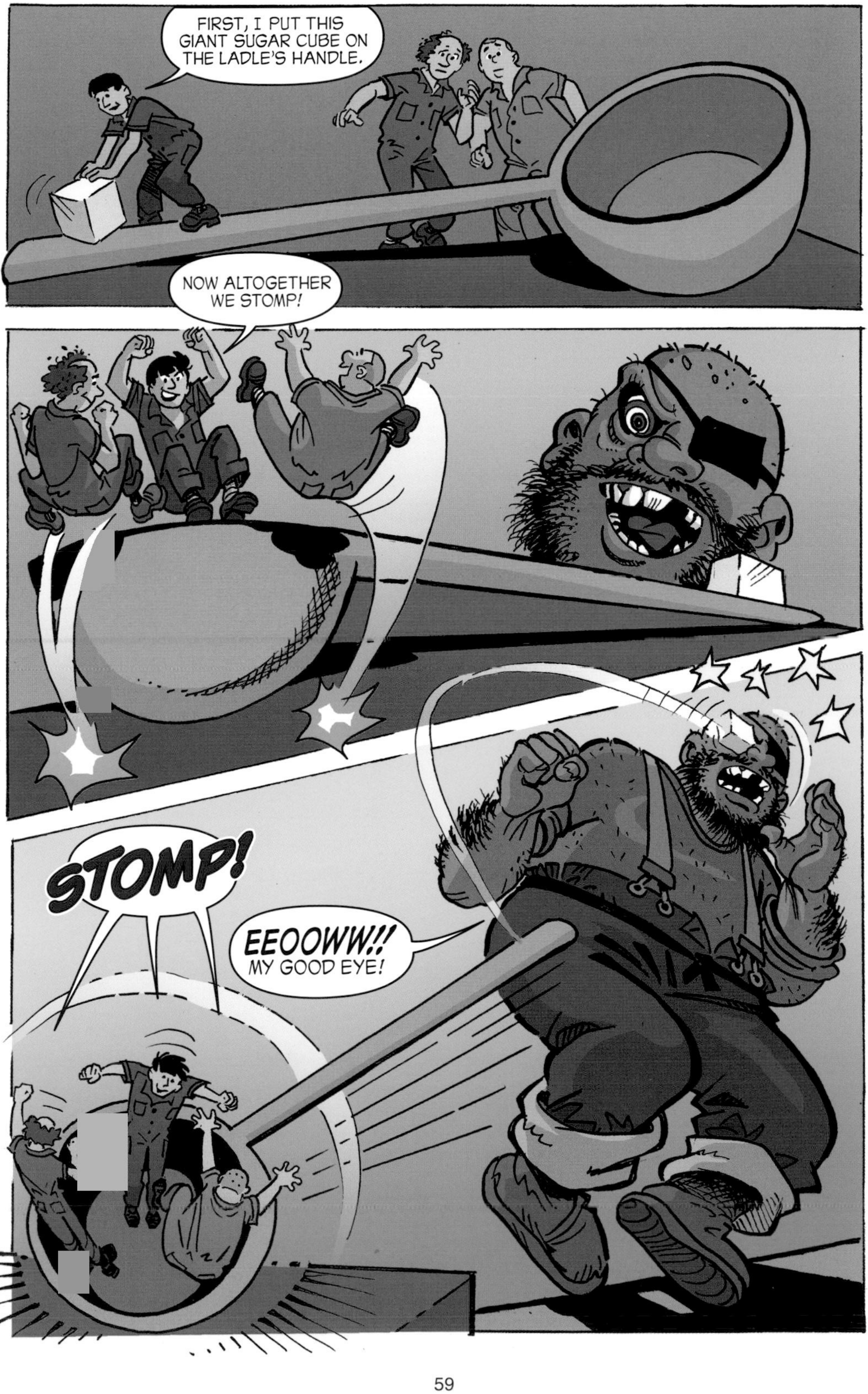
FIRST, I PUT THIS GIANT SUGAR CUBE ON THE LADLE'S HANDLE.
NOW ALTOGETHER WE STOMP!
STOMP!
EEOOWW!! MY GOOD EYE!

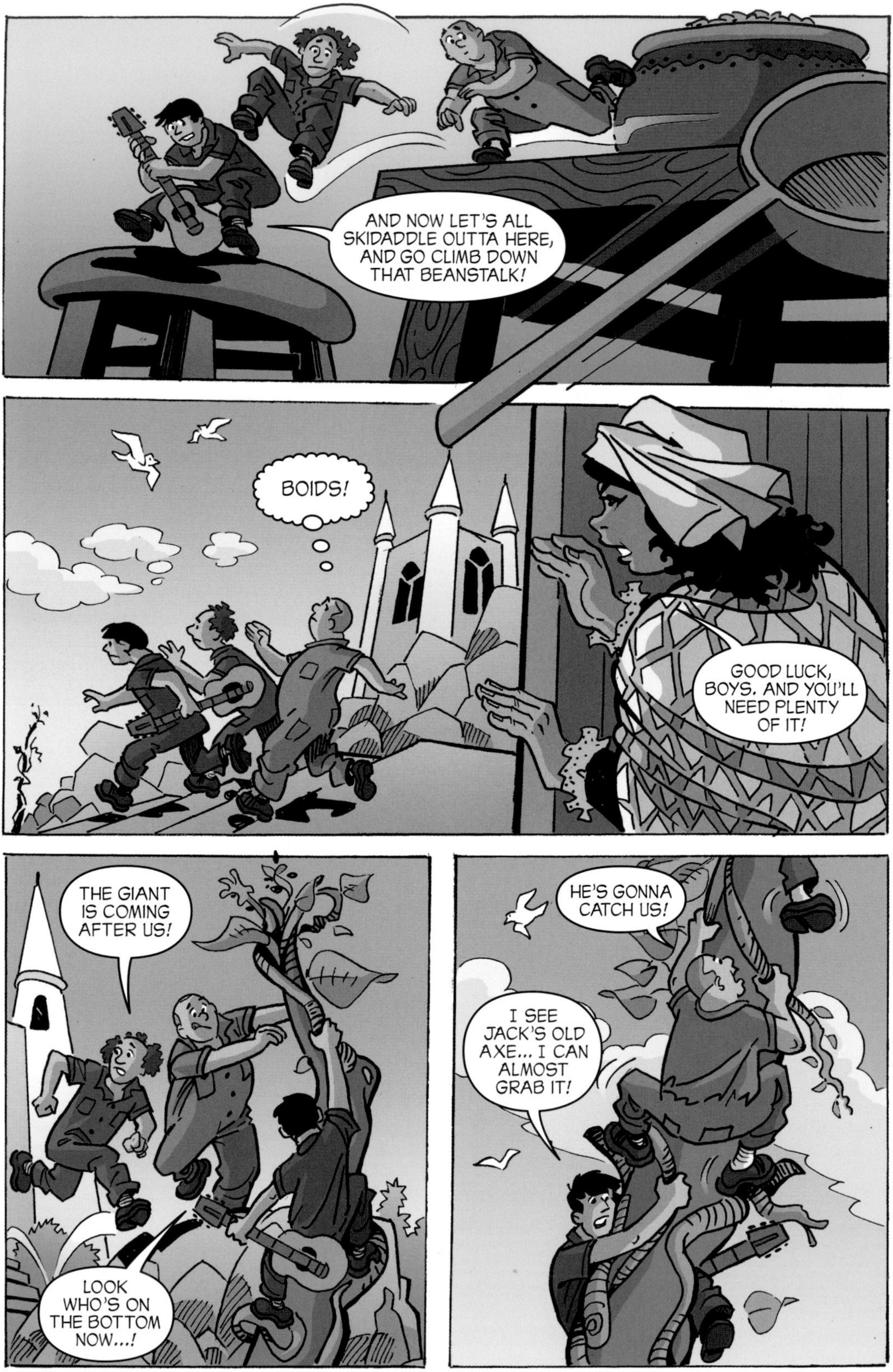
AND NOW LET'S ALL SKIDADDLE OUTTA HERE, AND GO CLIMB DOWN THAT BEANSTALK!
BOIDS!
GOOD LUCK, BOYS. AND YOU'LL NEED PLENTY OF IT!
THE GIANT IS COMING AFTER US!
LOOK WHO'S ON THE BOTTOM NOW...!
HE'S GONNA CATCH US!
I SEE JACK'S OLD AXE... I CAN ALMOST GRAB IT!

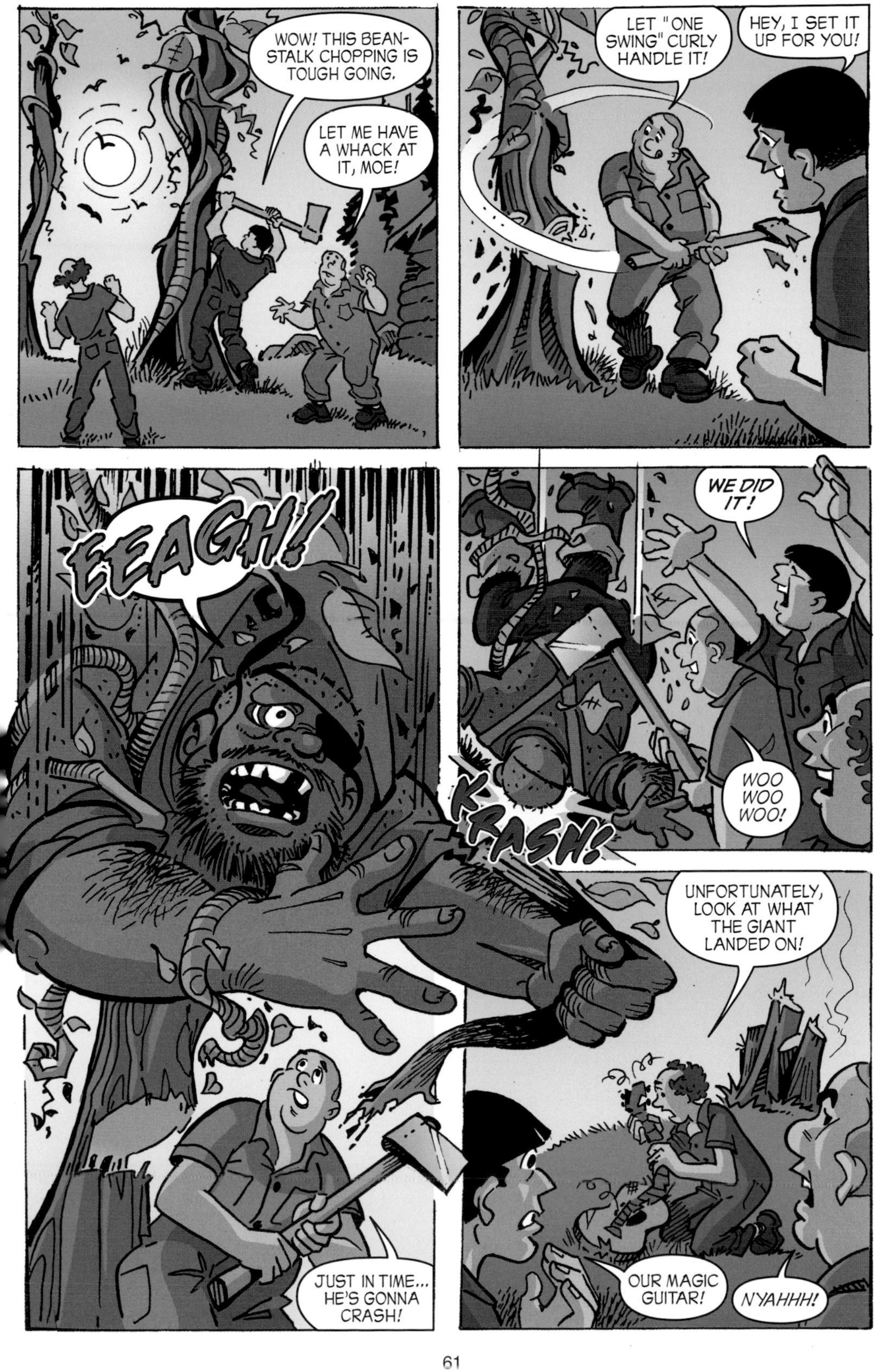
WOW! THIS BEAN-STALK CHOPPING IS TOUGH GOING.
LET ME HAVE A WHACK AT IT, MOE!
LET "ONE SWING" CURLY HANDLE IT!
HEY, I SET IT UP FOR YOU!
EEAGH!
KRASH!
JUST IN TIME... HE'S GONNA CRASH!
WE DID IT!
WOO WOO WOO!
UNFORTUNATELY, LOOK AT WHAT THE GIANT LANDED ON!
OUR MAGIC GUITAR!
NYAHHH!

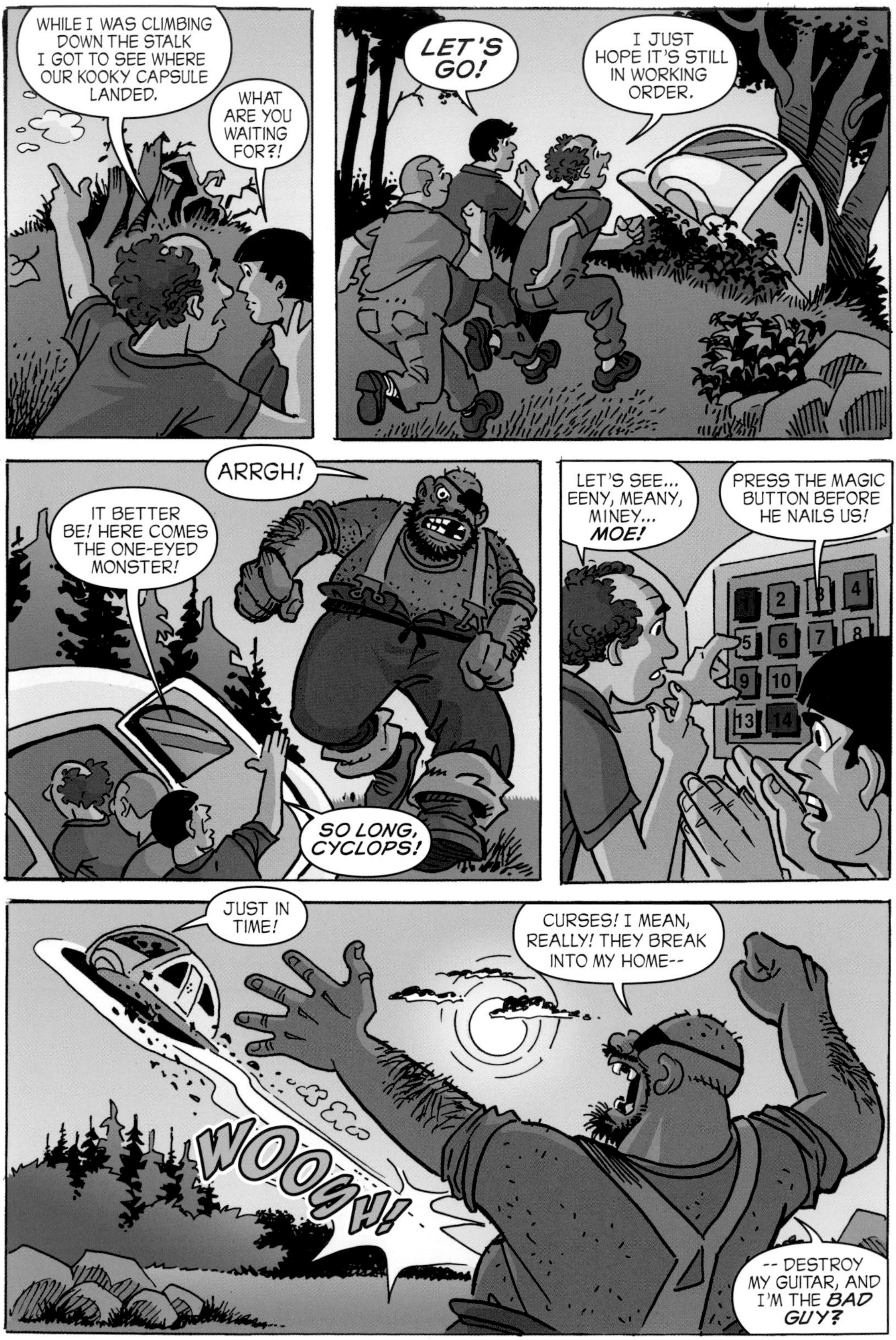
WHILE I WAS CLIMBING DOWN THE STALK I GOT TO SEE WHERE OUR KOOKY CAPSULE LANDED.
WHAT ARE YOU WAITING FOR?!
LET'S GO!
I JUST HOPE IT'S STILL IN WORKING ORDER.
ARRGH!
IT BETTER BE! HERE COMES THE ONE-EYED MONSTER!
SO LONG, CYCLOPS!
LET'S SEE... EENY, MEANY, MINEY... MOE!
PRESS THE MAGIC BUTTON BEFORE HE NAILS US!
1
2
3
4
5
6
7
8
9
10
13
14
JUST IN TIME!
CURSES! I MEAN, REALLY! THEY BREAK INTO MY HOME--
WOOSH!
-- DESTROY MY GUITAR, AND I'M THE BAD GUY?

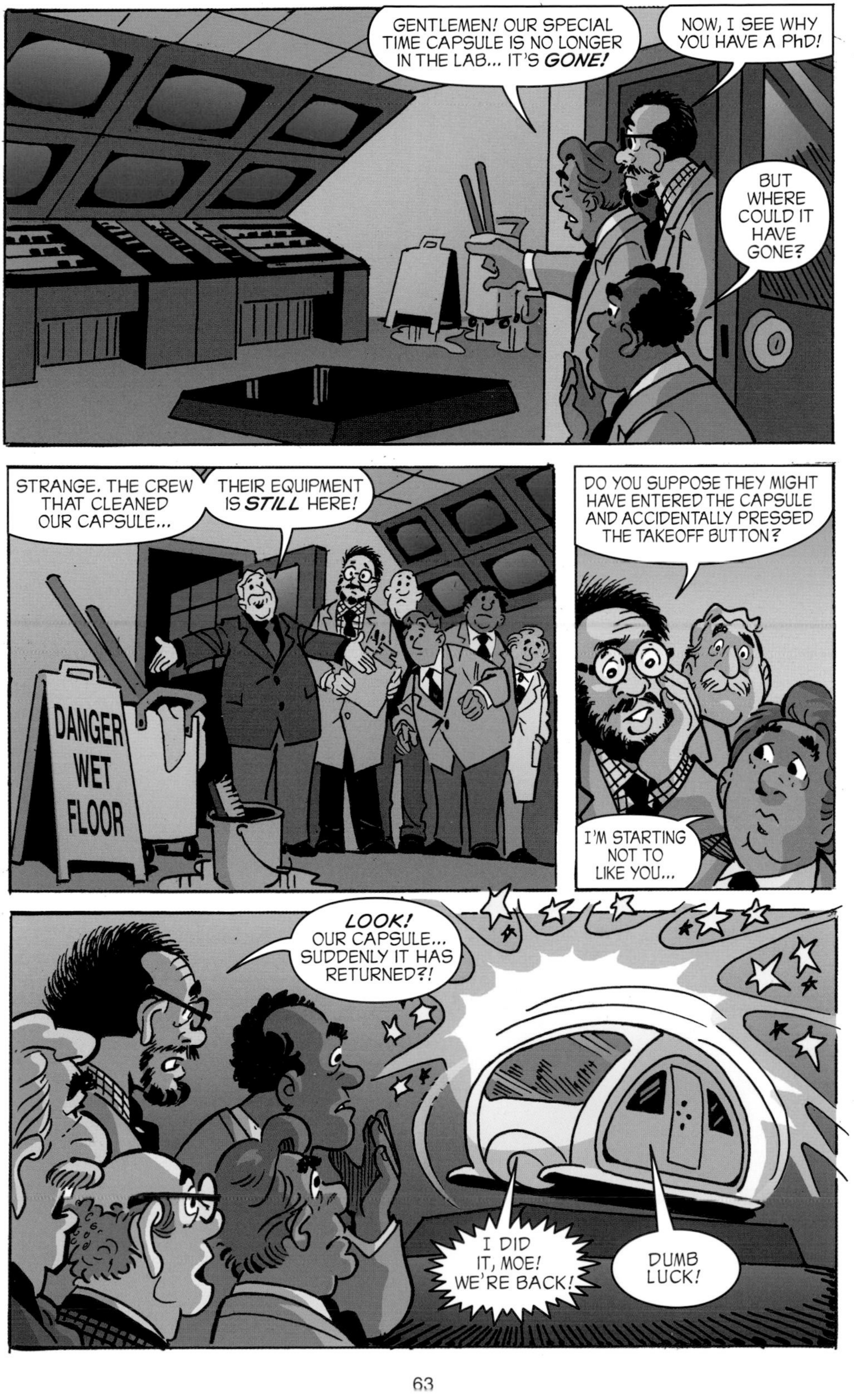
GENTLEMEN! OUR SPECIAL TIME CAPSULE IS NO LONGER IN THE LAB... IT'S *GONE!*
NOW, I SEE WHY YOU HAVE A PhD!
BUT WHERE COULD IT HAVE GONE?
STRANGE. THE CREW THAT CLEANED OUR CAPSULE...
THEIR EQUIPMENT IS *STILL* HERE!
DANGER WET FLOOR
DO YOU SUPPOSE THEY MIGHT HAVE ENTERED THE CAPSULE AND ACCIDENTALLY PRESSED THE TAKEOFF BUTTON?
I'M STARTING NOT TO LIKE YOU...
LOOK! OUR CAPSULE... SUDDENLY IT HAS RETURNED?!
I DID IT, MOE! WE'RE BACK!
DUMB LUCK!

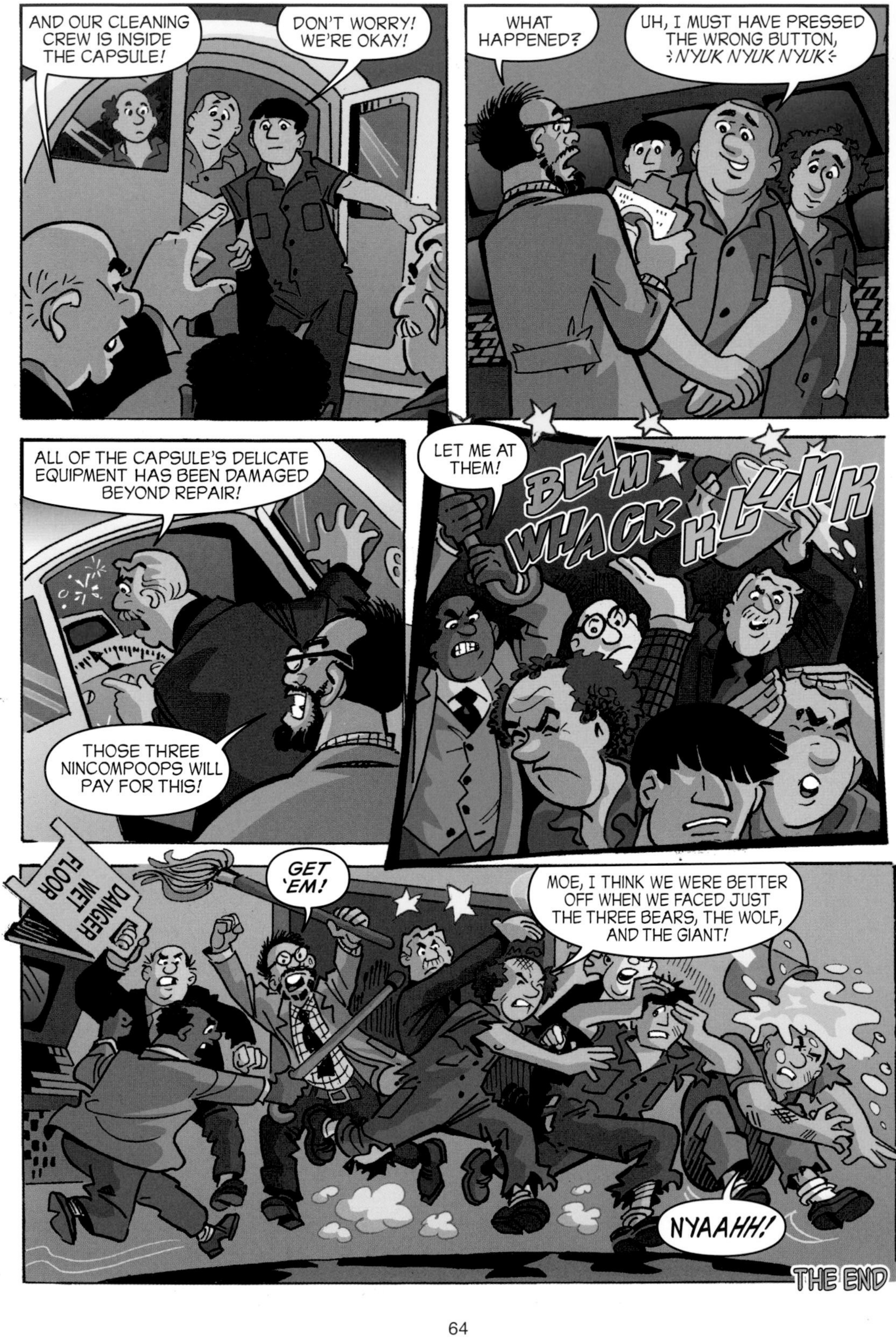
AND OUR CLEANING CREW IS INSIDE THE CAPSULE!
DON'T WORRY! WE'RE OKAY!
WHAT HAPPENED?
UH, I MUST HAVE PRESSED THE WRONG BUTTON, NYUK NYUK NYUK
ALL OF THE CAPSULE'S DELICATE EQUIPMENT HAS BEEN DAMAGED BEYOND REPAIR!
THOSE THREE NINCOMPOOPS WILL PAY FOR THIS!
LET ME AT THEM!
BLAM
WHACK
KLUNK
DANGER WET FLOOR
GET 'EM!
MOE, I THINK WE WERE BETTER OFF WHEN WE FACED JUST THE THREE BEARS, THE WOLF, AND THE GIANT!
NYAAHH!
THE END